LORD OF THE DEEP

LORD OF THE DEEP

GRAHAM SALISBURY

SCHOLASTIC INC.

New York   Toronto   London   Auckland   Sydney
Mexico City   New Delhi   Hong Kong   Buenos Aires

ISBN 0-439-54054-2

12 11 10 9 8 7 6 5 4 3 2   3 4 5 6 7 8/0

Printed in the U.S.A.   40

First Scholastic printing, April 2003
The text of this book is set in 11.25-point Trump Mediaeval.
Book design by Alyssa Morris

In honor of great teachers everywhere

Especially those in my life:

The Still Small Voice in my heart

James Monroe Taylor

Marion Grace Biscay

Thank you

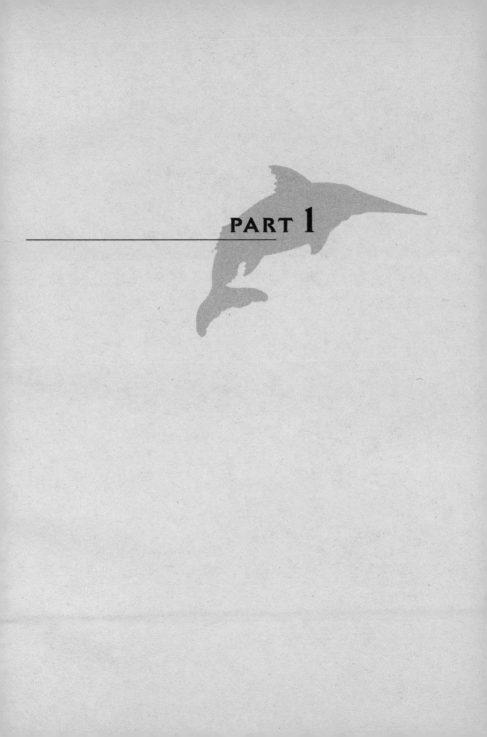

PART **1**

CHAPTER 1

THE ISLAND SLEPT.

Goats, pigs, dogs, chickens, mongooses.

Even the roaches and lizards.

Everything and everyone except Mikey Donovan, who was antsy as a rat to get up and get on down to the boat. He was thirteen years old and the youngest full-time deckhand ever to fish the deep waters of Hawaii's Kona coast. But Bill believed he could do the job. Mikey'd been working for three weeks now. And he couldn't get enough of it.

He lay with his eyes open.

His sheet was a twisted mass around his feet. The air inside his room was stuffy and humid, even in the high country where they lived. Nothing moved but a single tendril of sweat, creeping from his hairline to his ear.

He swiped it away with the palm of his hand.

This is crazy, he thought.

He picked up his clock.

Almost five.

Just get up. Bill would thump on his door to wake him soon, anyway. He rubbed his eyes and stood and peered out the window. The moon was bright white and low in the sky. A silver sheen illuminated the black sea beneath it.

In the bathroom he turned on the light and stood squinting at himself in the filmy, toothpaste-speckled mirror. Yeah, he thought, studying his practiced squint and darkening skin. Finally starting to look like a fisherman.

Thump!

Mikey jumped at the sound. Bill, waking him.

He brushed his teeth quickly and ran a wet comb through his hair, then dressed in a pair of khaki shorts and a T-shirt that read CRYSTAL-C in a blue arc across the front, with a picture of a leaping marlin under it and DEEP-SEA CHARTER FISHING under that. And below, in smaller print, BILL MONKS, SKIPPER.

Mikey turned off the light and went out to the kitchen. The light was on, but no one was there.

He peeked out the screen door. Bill was over in the

carport pouring oil into the outboard engine. Mikey eased the door back quietly.

He got a glass of orange juice and a bowl of Shredded Wheat and sat at the kitchen table, wondering where his mom was. She was almost always awake by now.

The screen door squeaked open.

Mikey glanced up.

"Morning," Bill said. He closed the door gently so it wouldn't slap shut. "Sleep well?"

"Yes sir."

Bill nodded and went over and got the coffeemaker going, then poured himself a glass of juice and sat across from Mikey. He broke three Shredded Wheat biscuits into a bowl. Before Bill, Mikey'd eaten nothing but sugary cereal. His mom didn't like it, but she'd never said no. Bill wouldn't touch the stuff. Rot your teeth, he said. Weaken your body. So Mikey stopped eating it.

They ate in silence, both studying separate spots on the tabletop.

"Where's Mom?" Mikey said.

Bill gulped his orange juice, his Adam's apple bobbing. He set the glass on the table. "Billy-Jay had a bad night. She was up with him."

"Is he all right?"

Bill hesitated. Mikey could tell he was concerned. "I think so. Your mom's taking him to the doctor today, just to be safe."

Bill got up and took his bowl and glass to the sink. He rinsed them and wiped his hands on his shorts. "Want to peek in on him?"

"Yeah."

Mikey pushed his chair back and followed Bill through the dark house. Billy-Jay was Mikey's three-year-old brother. Half brother, really, but Mikey didn't like to think of him that way.

The bedroom door was ajar. Bill put a finger to his lips and eased it open.

Billy-Jay really was a miracle, Mikey thought. You'd have to be if you were only three pounds when you were born. He could fit into Mikey's hand like a mango—if Billy-Jay had been strong enough to be held, anyway. At first he lived in a warm, clear plastic box, wired up with needles stuck into veins the size of a hair. Bill about wore himself out, sitting there for hours and hours in the hospital next to that box. Mikey could still remember him leaning forward with his elbows on his knees and his fingers laced together, worry lines carved deep into his forehead. Mikey'd seen those lines a lot in the past three years.

Moonlight brushed the walls of Billy-Jay's room. He slept with his blue blanket crumpled in his arms. It looked gray in the dim light. He's all Bill, Mikey thought. They looked so much alike it was weird.

Billy-Jay twitched once, but didn't wake. His breathing sounded a little raspy, but not too bad.

Bill tapped Mikey's shoulder and they left.

Back in the kitchen, Bill filled his dented silver Thermos with coffee for the boat and took it to the jeep.

Mikey followed him out, matching Bill's stride.

The air was crisp and smelled of mint, which grew wild along the edges of the yard. The sharp call of a distant rooster sliced the dark, jungled landscape.

Mikey glanced at the sky behind the mountain. Black turning purple. This was a time of day he liked, this dark stillness before dawn, when it was peaceful.

But Billy-Jay was still on his mind.

His breathing had been raspy when he was born. And he'd coughed a lot. Mom said he'd be fine, in time. But now he needed a lot of care. Mom had to quit her job. And though Bill could hardly work the boat alone, he finally had to let Frenchy, his deckhand, go because their health insurance didn't cover all the medical bills. That was what Mom said.

It was Mikey's idea to help on the boat. He'd been working up to it, anyway, learning things here and there from Bill, especially on the days Bill had no charter. "I'm thirteen now," Mikey said after Bill lost Frenchy. "I'm big enough and I already know the boat. And you don't have to pay me. I'll do it for tips. I can do the work, you know I can."

Bill said, "Think so?"

"Yes sir, I do."

Bill thought a moment, rubbing a hand over his mouth. Then he grinned and ruffled Mikey's hair. "Maybe you can, big guy, maybe you can. But it's hard work, you know. It's not just a boat ride."

"Yes sir, I know that."

"All right, then. Let's give it a shot."

Today was day fourteen.

Mikey blinked and turned when Bill moved an oil drum in the carport, making a harsh scraping sound. Bill unclamped the 10-horse outboard engine from the sawhorse he kept it on and took it and set it on the rear seat of the jeep. An old army jeep, no roof.

Mikey went over to the freezer in the carport and took out a rectangular five-gallon bucket of water frozen to ice. He turned the bucket over and let the ice fall to the concrete floor. Down at the boat he'd chop it up with an ice pick and spread the chips around in the drink cooler.

He took the empty bucket to a spigot and filled it with water and put it back in the freezer. Get it set and ready for the next day.

He wrapped the ice in an old burlap sack to slow the melting, then took it to the jeep.

"Get the beer and soda, too, would you, Mikey. And the water."

Mikey got the water, two six-packs of local Hawaiian beer, and two packs of root beer and Diamond Head strawberry soda from the cases Bill stored in a shed out behind the carport.

He remembered the lunches his mother had made for them the night before and went in to get them.

When he came back out, Bill was poking around in the dimly lit carport, picking through his lures, his tools, choosing what to take.

Mikey carried the lunches to the jeep, walking in the same slow way as Bill always did. It was hard not to mimic Bill. He'd been doing it for almost five years.

Mikey got in the jeep and waited for Bill as doves and mynah birds streaked across the darkness, flitting from tree to tree. A chaos of chattering, the way birds wake in the islands.

Bill slipped two looped wire leaders into the back pockets of his shorts and headed to the jeep. He slid behind the wheel and winked.

"Watch this."

He looked up at the trees, then clapped his hands once, loudly.

Instantly, the mass of chattering birds quieted. After a few seconds they started up again.

Mikey grinned.

Bill turned the key and let the engine warm up.

"Got everything?"

"Yes sir."

"Let's go."

CHAPTER 2

BILL KNOBBED ON THE HEADLIGHTS and drove up the steep driveway to the road. The engine growled, drowning out the birds. Gravel crunched and popped under the tires.

The headlights bounced in the bushes and trees that reached out over the bumpy old road that snaked down through the jungle to the harbor. It was barely wide enough for two cars to pass.

Bill drove slowly, taking his time, taking his time.

Down to the sea.

Down to the boat.

Mikey peeked over at him sitting so calmly behind the wheel, steering with one hand as if nothing at all were on his mind. His face was young and smooth, but the worry lines crossing his forehead made him look older. He's thinking about Billy-Jay.

Bill wore no hat, his dark hair combed straight back and his lean, suntanned muscles popping out of the sleeves of his T-shirt like molded clay. At twenty-seven, Bill wasn't really old enough to be Mikey's stepfather.

But that had never mattered.

Bill was the best.

Unlike his real dad.

Mikey snickered.

Real dad. Right. He wasn't a dad at all. He ran away sometime before Mikey was born, deserted him and his mom. Mikey guessed he just didn't want a son. Why else would you run?

Mikey put his hand out into the wind as they drove. The coolness felt good, and so did the warm metal floorboards under his bare feet.

Bill said nothing, so Mikey said nothing. It felt right; two men, going to work.

Back on Maui, before Bill, lots of guys had come around their sagging old green house on Ohelopapa Street. They'd wanted to see his mom, of course. Who didn't? She was beautiful—a dark-skinned Filipino–French Polynesian, and Mikey couldn't re-member a time when some guy or another wasn't fol-lowing her around. She was always kind to everyone, which, Mikey thought, wasn't always such a good idea. Some guys had a hard time taking a hint when things weren't working out.

But most of the time he and his mom had been happy, just the two of them in that old house.

Mikey smiled, remembering. He missed that place, hidden deep in a yard surrounded by a dense hibiscus hedge.

His old room was all wood—scuffed-up floors, scratched walls—single tongue-and-groove boards that only went up partway, then opened to the rafters and the underside of a corrugated iron roof. Mikey missed that roof almost more than he missed his best friend, Elroy. It didn't leak and it made great music in a rainstorm.

But he didn't miss his mom's old boyfriends. They were kind of weird. And they didn't really like it that his mom had a kid.

Just like his father.

Mikey tried to put him out of his mind. Why should he care anyway? Why should he even think about him?

Bill once said, "Try to forgive him, Mikey. Do that for yourself. He did the best he could."

Right.

"In fact," Bill added, "why don't you write him a letter? You never know, you might get something back."

Yeah, a big fat nothing.

His mom told him that his dad lived in Germany now, and that he'd come from a three-generation South Carolina military family. "He loved the army so much," she said. "But he was afraid of his father, and of *being* a father. He wasn't a coward, though, Mikey. You've got to believe that. He was in Special Forces, you know. The best of the best."

Mikey remembered staring at her and feeling nothing. "He ran away," was all he said, and Mom bit her lip.

"He was scared, honey. Just scared. He loves you. I *know* he does. Don't ever doubt that."

She was making that up so he wouldn't feel bad. Because if you really loved someone you wouldn't run away from them. For any reason. You would stay with them no matter what. Even if it was only a phone call once in a while. Something.

Write him a letter? Forgive him? Never.

Mikey was trying, though. Sort of.

But only because Bill said to.

Because he didn't really hate his father. He'd never even seen him. *Dad* was a word he hadn't used once in his life. Not once.

BILL AND MIKEY DROVE through the silent village that edged the bay. Ghostly gray fishing boats slept at their moorings out in the dark harbor. The ocean was calm, and no waves thumped up against the sea wall.

They parked on the pier and got out.

Bill took the small outboard off the backseat and stood waiting for Mikey with the 10-horse hanging from his fingers. He dipped his head toward the burlap bag. "Why don't you start taking care of the ice from now on?"

Mikey nodded and took the ice out of the burlap. He tossed the bag back in the jeep and raised the ice to his shoulder on the palm of his hand, the way Bill always carried it, like a waiter with a tray.

"Let's go," Bill said.

Mikey followed him, walking in the slow fisherman way. It wasn't far, maybe thirty or forty yards.

When they'd gotten about halfway to the skiff, his hand started feeling as if it were on fire. It froze so badly it burned. He switched hands, then ended up carrying the ice cradled in both arms, nestled against his chest, soaking his T-shirt.

Bill glanced back once, smiled, and kept on going.

Mikey juggled the ice from one side of his chest to the other, his whole upper body screaming with pain. He had to set it down on the hood of a truck—just for a second—while he jumped up and down with his hands buried in his armpits.

When he got to the skiff, he dropped the ice onto the floorboards and jammed his hands into the warm ocean and let them sting until he could move his fingers again.

Bill clamped the outboard onto the transom and fired up the 10-horse. He let it idle, smoky and loud.

Mikey fumbled, trying to untie the mooring line with stiff fingers. When he got the skiff untied he turned back and nodded to Bill.

"Look," Bill said, holding out his hand. "Feel that."

Mikey pressed his thumb into Bill's palm. It was tough as a coconut husk.

"Another month and your hands will toughen up. Then you can carry it," Bill said, trying to keep from grinning.

"Yeah, right," Mikey said.

They headed away from the pier.

PART 2

CHAPTER 1

THEY BUZZED OUT into the harbor in the skiff, slipping between the hulks of shadowy charter boats moored in the bay.

The ocean was dark and flat, with low swells that rolled in and undulated over the rocky shore. Three all-night yard lights at the hotel across the bay shot liquid golden spears over the glassy water, and Mikey could think of no other place on earth he'd rather be than here, heading out in the skiff with Bill to get the boat.

When they reached the mooring, Bill cut the engine and let the skiff bump against the stern of the boat. *Crystal-C* in black script swept across the transom, shadowed in gold.

Bill tilted the outboard up and locked it in place. "Take her forward," he said, then grabbed the ice and climbed aboard the *Crystal-C*.

Mikey stood in the skiff and moved it hand over hand along the gunnel to the buoy. He tied it off with the knot Bill had shown him, the bowline. The rope was wet and salty and rough. He tied it quickly, having practiced the knot many times at home before trying it on the water.

Mikey pulled himself aboard the big boat.

Bill started up the *Crystal-C* and let her idle. The engines rumbled in the silent bay, bubbly exhaust gurgling off the stern.

Mikey watched him in the lighted cabin, moving around, taking the rods out of their ceiling mounts and setting them on the bunk, checking them over. Getting things ready.

Mikey knew every inch of this boat. He'd crabbed along her edges, even crawled down into the bowels where the dank odors in the bilge made him dizzy. She was forty feet of sleek white fiberglass, with two towering outriggers, a deck above the cabin that Bill called a flying bridge, and in the engine room twin Detroit 450-horse marine diesels. A big boat with big payments, Bill joked.

Bill stuck his head out the cabin window. "Let's take her in."

Mikey, still on the bow, untied the *Crystal-C* and tossed the mooring line down into the skiff.

He turned and nodded to Bill.

Bill throttled up and swung the boat around, standing at the wheel in the dim yellow cabin light. Lord of the deep. It was kind of a joke, but that's what Mikey called him, because as far as he was concerned, Bill was the best deep-sea charter-fishing skipper there was.

Mikey took up the neatly coiled dock line and stood with it in his hands. Like springs, his knees rode the easy rise and fall as Bill walked the boat toward the pier.

Mikey breathed deeply, sucked in the salt air. For long moments he studied the fishing boats in the bay as the *Crystal-C* eased past. *Marjorie-Ann. Iwalani, Tiara, Magic, Lynell.* My boat will be moored here someday. Maybe I'll drop a hunk of concrete out near Bill's, hang my buoy there. Mikey wondered what he'd name his boat. So far he liked *Kaiolohia,* which meant calm sea, as in the early morning.

One light illuminated a circle of concrete, a single bulb under an aluminum reflector high on a post. Its yellow glow made Mikey imagine boats and oceans and faraway ports of call.

Back in Lahaina before Bill, his world was different. Near the sea, but not of it. There he had two good friends, Ricky and Elroy, and his mother and a black cat named Raisin. He had a grandmother, too, but she lived on Kauai, another island.

Then Bill came and everything changed. Mikey'd liked him right away, mostly because of two things.

The first was, when Bill came over to see his mom, he actually sat down with Mikey and talked to him—asked how he was doing in school, what his friends were like, did he like surfing, and, of course, was he a fisherman. The other guys that came around never did that.

And two, Bill took him out on the *Crystal-C*. Right after he met Mikey's mom, Bill said to him, "Come. We go holoholo. Take out the new boat. Just us men. What do you say?"

Mikey smiled, remembering.

Just us men. He'd never forget that.

Bill edged the boat up to the pier on the starboard side, facing the ocean. Mikey jumped off with the bow line and secured it to a black cleat.

The *Crystal-C* had been chartered for three days straight by two brothers from Colorado, Cal and Ernie Flynn. Yesterday was the first day, and they'd caught nothing. Skunked. That happened to everyone, even the best. Fishing was like that. But these guys wanted action, and it worried Bill, because they were the kind who'd come back year after year to charter his boat—if the fishing was good.

They were big guys, in their late thirties, Mikey guessed. This was their first time in Hawaiian waters.

Mikey liked them well enough. Sort of. They were kind of weird. One of them drove you crazy with his really bad jokes. But they told stories about elk hunting in Utah, freshwater fishing in Alaska, river running in the Grand Canyon, and rattlesnake hunts in the Arizona desert. They stretched the truth by miles, Mikey had no doubt about that. But so what?

Today Cal, the older brother, would be bringing his daughter along. Mikey looked forward to having a little kid aboard. He could tell her stuff he'd learned from Bill.

Mikey went about readying the boat as Bill had taught him to do—wiped salt off the windows and morning dew off the seats and the fish-fighting chair with a clean towel, chopped up the ice for the drink cooler.

Bill studied his drawer of lures, setting some aside.

Mikey looked up when Eddy Shin and his garbage truck came grinding out onto the pier. The truck crashed and banged and mashed the contents of the pier Dumpster into its belly, then headed over toward the *Crystal-C*.

Eddy shut off the headlights and the engine and got out. His neck was as wide as his head, and his arms were so packed with muscle they stuck out to the side when he walked toward the boat.

He grinned, looking down on Mikey with his gloved hands on his hips. "Shee, how come one runt kid like you got a job on this fine boat, huh, you tell me that?"

"Because I'm good," Mikey said.

Eddy laughed. "I believe it." He grabbed the starboard outrigger and stepped down onto the boat. "Where's the boss?"

"Down in the engine room."

Eddy pulled off a glove and reached out to Mikey. "So how's it going?"

Mikey shook Eddy's huge, rough hand. "All right, I guess. Except the guys we're taking out are kind of weird."

"Like what?"

"I don't know. Bossy. One of them tells really dumb jokes."

Eddy shook his head. "That's why I like my job, yeah? Don't have to deal with guys like that. So what you been catching these days?"

Just then Bill came up the companionway. "Hey, Eddy. What's new?"

"Well, seven fat papio, that's new. Caught 'em down Keauhou last night. Best fishing I had in a month."

"Using what?"

"Black squid lure."

Bill nodded.

Mikey wondered what the black squid lure looked like. And what it was like casting off the rocks at night. He'd seen guys out along the coast with torches.

Eddy said, "I hear you got some bozos on board today."

"Yeah, but they chartered the boat for three days straight. They said next year maybe they'll book us for five days." Bill shook his head. "But we got skunked yesterday."

"That happens, sure," Eddy said.

"They want marlin."

Eddy nodded. "That's why they come, yeah?"

"Problem is, it's quiet out there."

"You should try live bait, what Black Bart used to do. Catch 'em all day long."

"He was before my time. But I've heard of him."

"I think he's in Florida now. But man, the guy could bring in marlin like no one I ever saw in my life. Four, five, six hundred pounds. When every other boat was getting nothing, he still caught 'em. The guy was unreal. His first year he caught eighty-seven swordfish, eighty-seven! Chee. That's what, six a month? Seven? Lucky if you get three a month."

Wow, Mikey thought. You'd get anglers from all over the world with a record like that. You could make a fortune. And talk about building a rep. Jeez.

"Make sure the rods and reels are good and dry, would you, Mikey?" Bill tossed Mikey a fleece mitt.

Mikey slipped it on.

"So what you going do about these guyses' big fish?" Eddy said.

"I still got today and tomorrow. If I get skunked three days in a row, I might as well sell the boat, huh? But we'll see some action. I can feel it in my bones, something good."

Eddy ruffled Mikey's hair. "With a deckhand like this, how could you lose?"

"Can't."

"I heard you hired somebody, but I didn't know it was Mikey."

"I didn't think he'd be ready for a while yet. But he's proving me wrong."

Eddy made a fist and Mikey tapped it.

"How's little Billy?" Eddy said to Bill.

Bill looked down, then up. "He's doing fine."

"You making ends meet?"

"Yeah . . . thanks to Mikey. He's working for tips."

Eddy clapped a hand on Mikey's shoulder. "You one lucky man, Bill Monks."

"I got a whole family of luck, Eddy."

Eddy nodded and looked across the water toward the lights on the other side. "Well," he said. "Gotta go. Hey, Mikey. How's about sometime I take you night fishing? Show you how for catch papio?"

Mikey grinned. "Yes sir, that'd be great!"

"Fine. I call you up."

"But I don't have a spinning rig," Mikey said.

"I give you one. I got six."

"Really?"

Eddy glanced up at Bill. "I think this boy going be one of us, yeah? Look his eye. See that light? One of us, all right."

Eddy tapped Mikey's shoulder, then lumbered off the boat. Mikey could have hugged him, garbage smell and all.

CHAPTER 2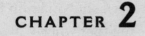

MIKEY STOOD with the fleece mitt on his hand. In the dim morning light he saw three people walking along the seawall. Cal and Ernie. And some lady?

This was Cal's daughter?

Huh.

As she approached he saw that she was more like his own age, or a little older.

Bill put his hand on Mikey's shoulder. "Now listen, I want you to talk with Cal's daughter today. Don't just go off and sit by yourself. Make sure she has everything she needs, all right?"

"Yes sir."

"Good. What we're doing now is trying to build a

relationship with these men. You'll understand what I mean when you get your own boat."

Mikey quickly wiped down the fishing rods that Bill had set on the bunk. He threw the mitt into a drawer. Keep busy, he thought. Don't just stand around looking like you don't know what you're doing.

He picked up the length of loose rope he'd been trying to splice into a loop for the past two days. Bill had been showing him how. It would be cool to be seen doing that when Cal and Ernie arrived at the boat.

Mikey squinted, trying to get a better look at the girl. But she was hidden behind the men. He wondered if she'd be easy to talk to. Did she like fishing, or had she come along only because Cal made her come? He'd seen that before. Last week some guy's wife came along, but it was obvious that she didn't want to be there. She didn't say a word to anyone the whole day.

After they'd come close enough to see him splicing the rope, Mikey tossed it back into the drawer. He went over and snugged the starboard gunnel up against the truck-tire bumpers on the pier. Bill stood next to him with his arms crossed.

Cal and Ernie looked down on them.

"Mornin', Billyboy," Cal said.

Bill smiled and said, "Men."

Cal and Ernie wore shorts, leather deck shoes without any socks, and gaudy Hawaiian shirts Mikey wouldn't wear in a thousand years. In the gap below Ernie's chin was a chain with a shark's tooth hanging from it. He hadn't had that yesterday. Cal didn't have one of those, but he did have a gold ring with a red stone the size of a fish eye on his finger.

Cal was some kind of scout for a hunting and fishing club that could send more business to the *Crystal-C* than Bill ever dreamed of—if the boat could produce fish, of course. Well, it would.

Ernie had three white box lunches tucked under one arm. Cal carried the beer—two six-packs, same as yesterday. He stepped aside and turned to look back at the girl.

She was fifteen or sixteen, looked like, wearing jeans shorts, white canvas deck shoes with socks, and a blue tank top. Her hair was long, straight, and golden. It fell nearly to her elbows.

She was carrying a paperback book and a tablet of some kind. And a small pouch that looked like a purse.

Cal said, "Hold these a sec, would you, Ali?"

She tucked her things under her arm and took the beer from Cal.

Cal pulled a cigar from his shirt pocket and peeled away the cellophane wrapper, glancing around the pier as he did. He lit the cigar with a wood stick match, then crumpled up the cigar wrapper and dropped it.

Mikey watched it fall.

"Billyboy, Billyboy, Billyboy," Cal said, in a long sigh.

As an afterthought, he nodded to Mikey.

Mikey didn't miss that Bill ignored all the "Billyboy"s. Bill said that most of the time he got great anglers on the *Crystal-C*. But sometimes he didn't. He once told Mikey, "Just send whatever you don't like out the other ear." Then he laughed and added, "As long as they're paying the bill, of course."

The girl pursed her lips and stooped down. She grabbed the cigar wrapper, balancing the beer on her knee, then stood and jammed the wrapper into her pocket.

Cal let out a smoky puff.

He shook out the still burning match and flicked it over the boat into the water. With the cigar in the middle of his mouth, he said, "Fine day, fine day."

Bill smiled up at him. "I smell action today, men, I do smell some big action."

"Action would be a real good idea," Cal said.

Bill grinned.

Cal took the six-packs back from the girl and handed them down to Mikey. Mexican beer. Tecate.

Bill reached up for the box lunches.

Cal put a hand on the outrigger and stepped down onto the boat. Ernie followed in the same way.

Ernie dipped his chin to Mikey. "Get that on ice,

boy. Beer ain't no good warm. And bury 'em deep, you hear?"

"Yes sir, deep."

"All right."

Mikey glanced up at the girl, still on the pier.

She looked back at him. Not smiling, not frowning. Just looking.

Mikey took the beer to the cooler.

He wasn't sure how he felt about another pair of eyes watching over everything he did all day long.

The first bottle of beer he took from the carton slipped out of his hands. It clanked on the deck and rolled away.

"Jay-zus, boy, you want that thing to explode in somebody's face?" Cal said.

"Sorry, sir." Mikey grabbed up the bottle.

Bill held the stern line taut and reached up to help the girl aboard. She took his hand and stepped down onto the boat.

With five people aboard, the *Crystal-C* suddenly felt a whole lot smaller to Mikey. Out on the water, the deck of a boat was all the world you had. What was he going to say to this girl, anyway? What Bill would say? That didn't help, because he knew what Bill would say—all kinds of ocean stuff that Mikey still had to learn. Why can't we just go on out and fish? Who needs to talk? But Bill had said, "Charter fishing is as much about people as it is about fish, Mikey. Don't forget that."

Ernie rubbed his hands together. "Let's go. We're burnin' daylight."

Mikey glanced toward the mountain. Daylight was a while away yet.

The girl headed into the cabin, brushing past Mikey. Her eyes were blue, and so pale they surprised him. He wanted to stare at them. You didn't often see eyes like that. He tried to smile. Probably looks as fake as it feels, he thought.

Her face flushed slightly. She looked away, then sat at the table. She set the tablet down. And the book, *The Agony and the Ecstasy*. Mikey'd heard of it, but he didn't know what it was about. It was kind of fat.

Bill went to the wheel.

Out on deck, Cal stood gazing at the black silhouetted mountain above and beyond the village, rising into the purple gray sky. "We'd better catch something today, by God," he mumbled to Ernie. "This is . . . embarrassing."

"Ain't that the truth," Ernie said.

Mikey looked into the cabin to see if Bill had heard. If he had, you couldn't tell.

"Set her loose, Mikey," Bill called.

Mikey scrambled up onto the pier. He untied the bow line and threw it aboard, then ran aft and untied the stern line and tossed it down on deck. He leaned out over the gap between the pier and the *Crystal-C* and shouldered the boat away and jumped aboard.

Bill throttled up and headed out of the harbor.

The engines grumbled, sickly sweet diesel exhaust swirling up and into the stern cockpit. Cal stood looking back, his knees pressed up against the transom. Ernie sat on the fish box.

Mikey stepped up onto the starboard gunnel and quickly spidered his way forward. There he coiled the bow line and laid it neatly on the deck near the forward hatch cover.

He then worked his way aft and coiled and stowed the stern line, doing it all perfectly, doing his job.

He wondered if anyone had watched him.

CHAPTER 3

THE SKY TURNED A PALE GRAY VIOLET, and golden light fanned out behind the island. Soon the sun would burst up over the mountain and flow down onto the silver black sea and turn it blue, and the island would ripen to greens and purples and browns.

Behind the boat, the village grew small. Scattered lights along the shore winked like campfires. It wasn't possible that the world could be more beautiful than it was from a boat in Hawaiian waters, Mikey thought.

Well, from what he knew of the world, anyway.

Mikey shook his head.

Better get to work. What to do next?

Get the rods out and put them in their chrome holders. But which ones did Bill want to use? Every day was different. Bill made his choices by the weather, the currents, the shape of the terrain in his depth recorder. Even superstition.

Mikey went into the cabin.

"Which rods should I take out?"

"Let's run four lines for now," Bill said. "Two one-thirties and two fifties. I'll come back and pick out the lures in a minute."

Bill glanced over at Cal and Ernie, now at the table with mugs of steaming coffee, both of them squeezed onto the bench seats with the girl.

She looked bored, gazing out the window at the dark coastline. Or was she watching everyone in the window reflections? Watching him?

"I figured we might troll on out to the marlin grounds," Bill said. "That okay with you?"

Some fishermen wanted to get out to the grounds right off, go straight for the big fish. Bill thought that was a waste of ocean. Not far offshore there was a shelf where the currents often churned up a morning of exciting action. Smaller fish, but scrappy fighters. Some anglers, though, wanted swordfish—the other name for marlin—and nothing else. Big game.

"I guess," Ernie said. "You're the one supposed to know these waters."

Mikey studied Ernie, his big arms and balding head. Maybe these guys knew about lakes and streams, but they sure didn't know much about saltwater game fishing. They thought they did, but they didn't. They had no idea that they would never in their lives fish with a skipper more skilled than Bill Monks.

Ernie saw Mikey looking and said, "Hey, boy, got another one for you. Why do they put bells on cows? You know that one?"

Mikey shook his head.

"Because their horns don't work." He laughed at his own dumb joke as if it were the funniest thing he'd ever told.

Mikey half smiled. It was way too early for this stuff. Jeez.

"Mikey? The rods?" Bill said.

"Oh. Right."

When they'd gone out past the lighthouse, Bill brought the throttle down to trolling speed. He set the wheel on automatic pilot, then squatted below the bunk across from the table. He pulled out a drawer and went about choosing his lures.

Mikey came back in and watched closely. There was so much to learn, all of it steeped in mystery. Especially choosing the lures, which Bill called plugs. How they worked made no sense at all to Mikey, because none of them looked like any fish in the sea. They looked like toilet-paper holders. Fish ate fish, not toilet-paper holders.

Bill said the plugs weren't supposed to entice fish to eat them. They were supposed to enrage them. Marlin, especially, hated them and attacked them mercilessly. It made no sense at all, but it worked.

Bill picked out two straight-runners and two chrome-headed jets. He handed one of the straight-runners to Mikey. "Feel that."

Mikey took it. "Heavy," he said.

It was a lure that Bill had made himself. Mikey wouldn't have chosen it in a million years. It was nothing but a shiny chrome tube filled with lead. A wire leader ran to the hooks through a hole bored in its center. Its face was flat, looking kind of like a roll of silver dollars with a rubber skirt on it. Why would any fish want that? Why would it enrage them?

"See this flat head?" Bill said. "That keeps the plug running below the surface on a straight track, like a bullet. Not very many fishermen have faith in a plug like this, but it works."

"Works for what? Marlin?"

"Ono," Bill whispered. "They strike at anything, but straight-runners are their favorite. That's our secret, huh?"

Mikey nodded.

"Hit this thing like a lightning bolt, you watch."

"Don't worry."

Bill grinned. He checked the hooks and the rubber skirting that hid them. "Look. Here's the thing. The angle of the line and the flat head keep it digging in the water. That's what makes it run straight."

Mikey stored that away. Another secret.

He stood and followed Bill out onto the stern deck. Mikey staggered a bit as the boat lurched in the gentle swells.

The sun's glow brightened the sky behind the mountain. It wouldn't be long before it spilled over the top.

Mikey attached the two jets to the swivels on their leaders. Bill did the others, all the time studying the water.

Mikey was aware of the girl watching him. He wondered what her name was. Ali? Cal had called her that. Why hadn't anyone bothered to introduce her to him?

Focus on what you're doing, Mikey told himself.

Think. Learn something new.

Mikey watched every movement Bill made. When Bill stared into the wake, Mikey stared into the wake. "When you look at the water, don't just see water," Bill said. "See color for depth. See current, how it's moving. Read it, listen to your gut."

Bill set out the flatlines first, the chrome jets, dropping them one by one over the transom. There was some exact distance he wanted them to run behind the boat, and Mikey knew that was part of what made a skipper great—or mediocre.

Then Bill held up a straight-runner and checked the two giant hooks hidden in the rubber skirting, then checked the skirt itself, one more time. When he was satisfied, he dropped the plug overboard and let the line free-spool out. After a moment or two, he shut off the run, set the clicker on, and yanked one last bit of line off the reel.

"Watch it work in the wake. You'll know when it's placed right. You'll get a feel for it."

Mikey squinted. He couldn't even find the lure, let alone watch it. He thought he could see the little spurts of white water that looked like the lure. Maybe.

Bill set the other long line, then rubber-banded it to the stinger line on the outrigger and let go. The outrigger hoisted the line up and away so the shorter flatline could work under it and not get tangled.

Mikey wanted to ask when the lures should run straight. Or zigzag across the wake. Should they make bubbles? Should they dive and jump, or run deep and not come up at all?

But he didn't want to ask now and look like he didn't know what he was doing in front of Cal and Ernie, and especially the girl. He'd watch, do what Bill did. Learn like that.

Bill clipped a safety line from each rod socket to each reel. If a rig went overboard, they'd be able to haul it back. Then he went back to the wheel and took the boat off autopilot.

Mikey stood with his knees braced against the transom. He tried to study the action of the lures, but the girl was still on his mind.

Talk to her.

But what about?

Nothing came to him.

He crossed his arms and studied the wake. It was hypnotic, flowing out and out and out, roiling with bubbles, smooth in the center, and the plugs making little spurts of ocean every now and then.

The sun broke over the mountain and dropped color down onto the sea. Mikey turned his face to the warmth.

The engines droned.

He glanced into the cabin.

Cal and Ernie had taken out a deck of cards. Cal was shuffling them, bridging them in the depths of his palms and releasing them, then banging the edges on the table and doing it all again.

The girl now stood in the aisle, facing aft.

Her eyes met Mikey's.

She tilted her head, slightly.

Mikey smiled and looked away.

He turned back.

She was still looking.

CHAPTER 4

MIKEY TURNED and scowled at the lures. "Take one," he whispered to the fish wandering the depths below.

Bill needed something to happen.

Something these guys could take home and talk about.

Mikey thought he saw a glistening black shape dart across the wake. He unfolded his arms and squinted.

Nothing.

But he was sure he'd seen something.

They trolled north, two miles offshore. The shape didn't return. It was one of those mysteries that would haunt him for hours, Mikey knew. Unless something hit the line; then every thought in his head would vanish instantly. That was how it was on the water: either it was so quiet and boring you just sat around trying to stay awake, or it was so exciting you almost forgot to breathe.

That was deep-sea fishing.

Mikey went into the cabin, passing Cal and Ernie and the girl, who was now sitting on the bunk across from them.

"How you doing, honey?" Cal said to the girl. "Feeling okay? Not getting queasy, are you?"

"Why'd you think I'd be getting queasy?" she said.

"Oh, I don't know, just that you're a . . . you know . . . you're . . . you're not used to boats, and all."

She shook her head and looked back down at her book, which lay open in her lap.

Ernie said, "Ah, lighten up, Ali. Hey, listen. You hear about the idiot who got a camera for his birthday? He just got his first set of pictures back—twenty-four shots of his left eye. *Bwahahahahahah!*"

"That's lovely, Uncle Ernie," the girl said. "Was your next roll like that, too?"

Ernie laughed harder, slapping the table. Even Cal smiled. "Come on, Ernie, stop yakking and deal."

"All right, all right."

Mikey thought it was weird the way the girl talked back like that. These people were really strange.

Mikey checked the depth recorder. Forty-eight fathoms. While he watched, it jumped to seventy, then back to fifty-one. He figured Bill was following an undersea shelf. He made note of the coastline, looking for rock formations or tree clusters that he could use to pinpoint this trolling spot again, this shelf. A fisherman needed all the secrets he could collect.

He sat in the seat across from Bill with his back to the window. The hull rose and fell over the mild, easy-moving swells. He breathed deeply.

Bill glanced over and nodded.

The engines droned.

Bill dug out a chart and studied it, his forehead furrowed. He reached over and turned on the shortwave radio, which spat static over a small, faraway voice. Some Honolulu boat, fishing out near Penguin Bank.

Cal and Ernie played blackjack. Drinking slow morning beers. Smoking cigars. The smell was sharp and strong, but Mikey didn't mind it.

After a while, Ernie placed his cards facedown on the table and sat back. He took a deep pull on his cigar and let the smoke out around his words. "So, Billyboy, I'm kind of wondering where that action is. Can you give us a clue?"

"It'll come," Bill said.

"Marlin?"

"That's the idea."

Cal put his cards down, too, and turned in his seat to face Bill. "Guy at the hotel bar last night told me a story about some skipper here whose swordfish stuck its bill in the bottom."

Bill nodded. "That was a strange one, all right. He fought that fish for hours. Finally, it got so enraged it sounded, went straight to the bottom and stabbed its sword into the sand. Got stuck there."

Bill shook his head.

"Of course, on board they didn't know that. All they knew was the line was stuck. Well, that skipper was stubborn. Most guys would just cut the line and move on. But he didn't like losing a fish like that. So what he did was he pulled out his Aqua-Lung and went down to see what was going on."

"Not," Mikey said. He couldn't even imagine doing that.

"It's true," Bill said. "He went down to look. What he found was a dead marlin. Probably died of exhaustion and pressure. So the guy dug the sword out and went up and pulled the marlin aboard. It weighed in at over four hundred pounds. Now that's stubborn."

"What boat was that?" Cal said.

"He's long gone. That was a while back."

Cal pursed his lips. "Too bad."

"That kind of stubborn is what it takes, ain't it?" Ernie said.

Cal picked up his cards. "Yup."

CHAPTER 5

THE CHROME CLOCK above the companionway clanged the half hour. Mikey watched the minute hand click forward. One stiff step, then another.

He glanced back at the girl.

She was sitting cross-legged on the bunk. The notebook she'd brought was a sketchbook. The purselike thing held pencils and a black-ink drawing pen, which she was using now. Mikey couldn't see what she was drawing, but he watched her movements, loose and fast. Was she any good?

She glanced up just as he stretched his neck to get a better look.

He shifted his eyes, pretending to look beyond her. At the rods, maybe. Or the lures, jumping in the wake.

"Why we staying so close to shore?" Cal said suddenly, now back to his cards.

"Philosophy," Bill said, and grinned.

Cal looked up. He gazed over his shoulder at Bill. "What the devil's that supposed to mean?"

Bill turned down the radio static.

"Some guys like to race on out to the marlin grounds. Set out the lines when they get there, start trolling. Go straight for the big ones. But they do that, they miss out on some of the best fighting fish you can find in these waters. They're just smaller, is all. But they give you your money's worth, all right."

Cal *humphed* and turned back.

Ernie, hunched over his cards, said, "Well, I guess we're in the right place, then, because we could sure use our money's worth."

Bill said nothing.

The skin at the corner of his eyes was already cut with the lines of permanent squint. Real fishermen fish. Fake ones wear mirror sunglasses and white hats. Bill never wore a hat, or sunscreen, and sometimes not even his T-shirt.

Cal slapped some cards on the table. "Gimme three."

Ernie gave him three cards.

"You boys know what an ono is?" Bill asked.

Ernie said, "It's a wahoo, right?"

"That's it. Looks like a barracuda. Good fish to

fight, good fish to eat. You find those right around here, close to shore. But the best fighting fish in these waters is mahimahi. That's a fisherman's fish. In my opinion."

"Marlin," Cal said. "*That's* a fisherman's fish. In my opinion."

Bill nodded. "We'll give them a shot, too."

"Hey, boy," Ernie said. "Grab me a beer, would you? And not one of your local rotguts."

Mikey jumped up, went aft, and dug around in the cooler for one of the Mexican beers, buried deep. He liked the Spanish printed on the label. He pried off the cap, wiped the bottle dry with a towel, and took it to Ernie.

Just as Ernie reached for it, one of the reels screamed. The rod bowed out over the water, jerking and jumping in its holder.

Bill throttled down, then leaped out of the pilot's seat and rushed aft. Mikey leaned into the table to let him pass, then raced after him.

Cal and Ernie dropped their cards and scrambled out of their seats. The girl hugged the sketchbook to her chest.

"Mikey!" Bill shouted.

Mikey knew what Bill wanted and ran to release the stinger on the port outrigger. He started reeling in the lure, keeping the rod in the rod socket.

It was the port flatline that had been hit. The pole

leaped and bobbed. The clicker kept screaming, the wailing oh so sweet in Mikey's ears.

The boat rocked in the sea, inching slowly forward while they got the lines in. The noise of the engines had dropped to a gurgle. Exhaust bubbled up into the cockpit, making Mikey's stomach turn.

The girl came out and stood one step up on the chrome ladder to the flying bridge. She held her hair aside with one hand.

"Who's up first?" Bill shouted.

Mikey knew Bill was anxious to get someone to take up the rod and start working the fish before it took half the line off the reel.

"Ali," Cal said, turning to the girl. "You take this one."

She backed up the ladder. "I don't want to."

Bill madly reeled in the starboard flatline to get that lure out of the water. He glanced over his shoulder. "Someone take the rod out and sit in the chair!"

The girl didn't move.

Cal grabbed the rod and pulled it out of the socket. He yanked it back to strike the fish, sink the hook deeper. "Come on, Ali. It's why we're here."

"I said I don't *want* to."

The reel jumped in Cal's hands, as if alive. He spread his feet apart and braced himself, the clicker still wailing.

Mikey finished bringing in the port long line. He

dropped the lure onto the gunnel, out of the way, then started in on the starboard flatline.

Bill shoved him aside. "I'll get this. You watch the wheel."

"Ali, for heaven's sake, give it a try," Cal said.

The girl shook her head.

Mikey ran in and slid behind the wheel and turned the boat so the line was directly off stern.

"Good God, give it to me," Ernie said.

He grabbed the rod from Cal and wrestled it back. He fell into the fighting chair and set the base of the rod into the chrome cup between his legs.

Mikey kept his eyes pinned on the action, looking back over his shoulder. It was his job to keep the line directly off the back of the boat.

No mistakes.

Ernie fumbled with the drag on the reel. The clicker was making a terrible racket as the fish ran with the bait. Bill stopped reeling in the flatline and reached over and shut the clicker off.

"Lot of line going out," he said, hoping Ernie would take the hint and start working the fish.

Ernie put his back into it, pulling, then reeling as he fell forward.

The initial run was fast and furious. But after Ernie started working it, the fish slowed. In minutes it seemed to have lost some of its fury. But its strength showed on Ernie's pinched and sweaty face when he turned to Bill. "What is this? Fights like a pit bull."

"Yes sir," Bill said, grinning.

Finally, the *Crystal-C* was producing.

Cal stood beside the chair, coaching. "Pull with your back, Ernie. Use your legs, that's what they're there for."

"I know what I'm doing!" Ernie snapped.

The fish ran to port. Mikey wheeled the boat to starboard, keeping the line where Bill wanted it, straight back. Some fishermen liked the line off to the side. Some even liked to wander around the boat, standing with the butt of the pole in a waist cup.

But Bill liked it this way.

While Mikey guided the boat, Bill grabbed the fish glove and the gaff, a three-foot pole with a barbless chrome hook on it, for pulling the fish out of the sea. He set them on the gunnel.

He stood at the transom, waiting.

Ernie worked the fish closer, pulling and reeling, pulling and reeling, taking line in inch by inch.

Ten minutes later the fish gave up.

As the leader rose from the water, Bill reached out and grabbed it with a gloved hand. He pulled the fish closer, hand over hand.

Mikey put the throttle in neutral and ran back.

Bill, and now Mikey, leaned over the transom, looking down into the depths. The gleaming blue and silver ono paced back and forth, swimming on its side with the line running up from its mouth.

"Got you a fine wahoo," Bill said.

Cal peered over the stern between them.

"Stand back," Bill said. "This fish has razor-sharp teeth. I don't want anyone getting cut up."

Cal moved back.

Ernie, still in the chair, pulled his feet up.

The girl climbed one step higher on the ladder.

Bill tugged the ono closer.

He gaffed it just behind the head, near the gills. The ono went crazy. It writhed and shook, churning the water white.

Bill dropped the leader and picked up the billy club. He lifted the fish out of the water just far enough to club its head—one, two, three, four times, good solid thumps.

Whock! Whock! Whock! Whock!

An ugly, hollow sound.

Whock!

One last time.

A live ono flipping around on deck could be big trouble.

The fish shuddered, and died.

With a grimace, his muscles wet and bulging, Bill hefted the ono up and over the transom, holding the gaff in both hands. He laid it on the deck so all could see.

"Keep back," he said.

Mikey ran to the six-foot fish box and tore off the foam seat cushion. He lifted the lid. With the ono still on the gaff, Bill carried the fish to the box and dropped it in.

Four feet long, about. Spiky teeth gleaming.

The girl came down off the ladder. Cal and Ernie— the rod still in his hands—crowded in to see the fish, long and slick and cobalt blue. A wahoo, with jutting jaw and shiny silver belly and dark vertical stripes along its flank.

The girl opened her mouth, but no words came out.

"Looks like he swallowed the hook," Ernie said. He looked at Bill. "How you going to get it out?"

"Pliers."

Bill closed the fish box.

"But first I'm going to let him be dead a little bit longer. Bring her up to speed, Mikey."

Mikey ran forward and throttled up to eight knots. He set the course toward open sea, then put the boat on autopilot and went back out into the stern cockpit.

"Beer, boy, three cold ones," Ernie said. "One for Cal, two for me, and make it fast. I'm sweatin' like a pig."

Mikey got the beers. Fast.

While Bill reset the lines, Mikey scooped a bucket of water out of the ocean and sloshed it over the deck, then scrubbed the floorboards clean with a long-handled brush. The water swirled and sloshed and funneled out a deck hole, bringing a welcome coolness. Mikey stowed the bucket and brush.

It wasn't all that big, the ono, maybe thirty-five or forty pounds. But it was a decent catch and it was safely stowed in their fish box. And Mikey'd kept the line just where Bill wanted it, he'd scrubbed down the deck and gotten the boat back up to speed.

The girl stood at the transom with her arms crossed, studying the wake. What was she was thinking about?

Cal drained his beer and tossed the bottle into the ocean. He looked at the back of the girl's head a moment, then went inside to the table and picked up the cards.

The girl climbed up to the flying bridge.

Bill took off his shirt and swiped it across his face and neck, then stuck it in his back pocket, where it hung like a tail.

Mikey took his shirt off, too. He wiped his face and stuck the shirt in his pocket in the same way Bill had. Nothing felt quite as good as doing your job the way it was supposed to be done.

They stood awhile, watching the water.

"I've been thinking, Mikey," Bill said, looking into the wake with his hands on his hips.

Mikey turned to look at him.

"What would you think about having a name like Mikey Monks?"

"What do you mean?"

"Change your last name."

"You can do that?"

"Little paperwork is all."

"Really?"

Bill turned and grinned. He brushed a hand over Mikey's hair. "You'd have to let me adopt you."

Wow.

"Just something to think about."

Bill looked at the lines one last time, gave Mikey a wink, then went back in to the wheel.

Mikey's gaze followed him.

When he saw Cal watching, he turned back to study the wake.

Mikey Monks . . . yeah.

The girl came into his mind. Why didn't she want to fight the fish? That was why you chartered a boat.

You can ask, he thought. You're supposed to talk to her.

Now's as good a time as any.

He climbed up to the flying bridge.

"Hi," Mikey said.

She gave him a look that said Yes?

Mikey hesitated. "Uh . . . how come you didn't want to catch that fish?"

"I don't like fishing."

"Oh."

He thought a moment.

"Well, why'd you come out with us today?"

"Does it really matter?"

Mikey wanted to go back to the lower deck. "Uh . . ."

Cal saved him by popping his head up from down below. He stood halfway up the ladder with a cold strawberry soda in his hand.

"Thought you might be thirsty, Ali," he said.

The girl glanced at him, then looked away. "I don't like strawberry."

Cal opened his mouth to say something more, but decided not to. He started back down the ladder.

"Wait!"

The girl reached out.

Cal smiled and gave her the can.

Cal left.

Mikey watched her take a long gulp.

"You don't get along with your father?" he said. Then wished he hadn't.

"What kind of question is that?"

"I don't know. Just seems like . . . well, like you don't like him . . . or something."

"He's my father. I have to like him."

Mikey nodded.

A moment later, the girl spoke, so softly Mikey could barely hear it. "My mother told him to take me, not that I wanted to go. 'Why don't you do something with your daughter for once?' she said. Just like that.

Right in front of me. And Dad looked surprised, like he'd never even thought of such a thing. Like, Are you kidding? How do you think that made me feel?"

Mikey thought before answering. "Kind of bad?"

"You got that right, Ace."

"So . . . why'd you say you wanted to go?"

"Because he asked me."

"But you didn't want to."

"I know."

Mikey frowned.

The girl smiled. It wasn't an angry smile, or a cynical one. It seemed real.

Mikey turned and gazed out over the sea.

Where it was clear.

Where it was simple.

He went back down to look for something to do.

Anything.

CHAPTER 6

AROUND TEN O'CLOCK they ran into an unbearable stench.

It was so bad that one accidental deep breath nearly made Mikey gag. He put his T-shirt back on and pulled the neck up over his nose.

"My God," Ernie said, "what *is* that?"

"Something's dead," Bill said.

Holding a towel over his mouth and nose, Ernie looked out over the ocean. "I don't see anything but water."

"It's out there."

"Well, get us away from it."

"Mikey," Bill said. "Go up on the flying bridge. See if you can spot where the stink's coming from."

Mikey took a gulp of air from inside his T-shirt and ran out. He scrambled up the ladder to the flying bridge, then covered his face again. The stench made him want to barf.

The girl was sitting cross-legged on the deck drawing in her sketchbook. The neck of her tank top was drawn up over her nose just as his was. She laughed when she saw him holding his shirt up, too.

"Uh . . . ," Mikey said, "I wanted to see if I could find where that smell was coming from."

The girl put her sketchbook down and stood up, still with the tank top over her face. "What is it?"

"Something dead."

Mikey spotted it off the starboard beam, maybe two hundred yards away. A whale. Its oil was slicked out around it, making the surface of the water as smooth as a silky lagoon.

"Yuck," the girl said.

Mikey grimaced. But the overwhelming repugnance captured him, drew him in. It was so powerful. So huge.

"Be right back," he said.

He slid back down the ladder navy-style and went in and pointed out the dead whale to Bill. Bill immediately altered course. "Been a while since I've seen that," he said.

Cal and Ernie wandered out on deck to get a better look. They both covered their faces with towels.

Mikey climbed back up to the flying bridge.

The *Crystal-C* skirted the whale and got upwind of the stench, the boat moving easily in the calm sea. Bill tracked back to get a closer look.

Mikey and the girl stood at the rail on the flying bridge, looking down on a sight that made Mikey's skin crawl.

Just beneath the surface, the carcass was engulfed in a frenzied mass of oceanic white-tip sharks, their round eyes vacant. They twisted and writhed and opened their ghastly jaws, leaving whirlpools of blood-ink on the water where they'd fought with each other or ripped meat off the bloated whale, releasing the inner rot that fouled the air.

Mikey stepped back.

The girl gasped. "Are those . . ."

"Deep-water sharks. You could throw the anchor overboard and they'd eat that, too. If you fell off this boat you wouldn't last five seconds."

The girl backed away, too.

"Sorry," Mikey said. "I don't mean to scare you."

"You don't. They do."

Mikey shuddered. "I can't think of a worse way to go."

The girl edged back to the rail. "Still," she said. "I think they're kind of . . . beautiful."

"Beautiful?"

"They have nice lines, nice shapes."

"And nice appetites."

"Have you ever been in the water with one? I mean with a shark?"

Mikey *humphed*. "Oh yeah."

"Where? What did it feel like?"

"It was a while back," he said, but didn't go on. The memory still scared him. A little. Enough.

It was when he lived in Lahaina, back before Bill. It wasn't the deadly breed of shark that was savaging the whale in front of them, but it was bad enough. Mikey had decided months later that he'd probably never been in any real danger, but he could have been. With a shark, you just never know.

"Well, what happened?" the girl said.

Should he tell it straight, or maybe add a little extra to make it sound better?

No, straight was good enough.

"I used to live in Lahaina. On that island over there." Mikey lifted his chin toward the faint blue outline of Maui off in the distance.

"One day I went snorkeling, looking for shells. I was eight. I'd just gotten a new snorkel and face mask for my birthday."

"When's your birthday?"

"In April."

"Mine's in August."

"Well, anyway, I took a screwdriver with me—in case I needed to pry a shell off a rock, or something. It was a really rough day. The whole coastline was nothing but white water. But there was a channel that I could get out through."

Mikey noticed how the girl listened. She seemed different up on the flying bridge, away from her father. More relaxed. She studied him intently, as if every word were of the greatest importance.

Mikey spoke slowly, liking it. No one had listened to him like that before, not even Bill or his mother.

"Well, anyway," he went on, "I . . ."

Mikey *really* liked the way her eyes never left him. She hardly even blinked. It made him want to . . . to puff up, or something. It made him feel really good.

"Okay," he said, "okay."

He took a breath.

"I swam out beyond the waves. The water was all churned up with sand and bits of seaweed. It was murky near the reef. But farther out it was clear."

He remembered that he was scared of getting raked over the reef by the waves. The ocean was wild and tossed him around when he got too close to the coral.

"Was your mom or dad on the beach? Watching you?"

Mikey raised his eyebrows. "No. . . . Why would they be? Anyway, I didn't have a dad then."

"But—"

"Bill's my stepdad. I still have my old last name, Donovan."

"Mikey Donovan. Nice. Well, anyway, it was dangerous and all. Wasn't it?"

"Nah. It was just kind of rough."

"So then what?"

"I swam around looking for shells and one time when I came up, for some reason I turned around. And I saw a shark fin. Behind me. Ho, did I freeze up. It was so close, only about the length of this boat away. Then the fin went under."

"Yow!"

He'd been scared, all right, but he wouldn't tell her that. "My first thought was, I gotta get out of the water. But the only way was to go back through that small channel. If I tried to go in over the reef, I'd get sliced to shreds on the coral."

Mikey stopped, remembering how his heart had nearly hammered out of his chest. It was the most scared he'd ever been in his life, even to this day.

"So what did you do?"

"The only thing I could do—I headed for the channel. But first, I went under one more time to look for the shark. It was gone. That was the worst, not knowing where it was."

"You must have been scared to *death*."

"I was," Mikey said, not caring now if she knew. "I nearly peed." He winced. "Sorry."

The girl giggled. "Don't stop now."

"Well . . . couple minutes later, the shark was there

again. I don't know where it came from, but there it was, right in front of me. Wasn't that big, maybe five or six feet. But it was bigger than *me*."

"Get out of here."

"No, really, it was."

They'd gotten downwind of the whale stench again. They pulled up their shirts.

"So then what?" she asked.

"Well . . . like before, I froze up. But lucky for me, the shark turned and swam away, and I started swimming over to the channel. I tried to go slowly, so I wouldn't splash a lot. They have bad eyesight, you know."

"They do?"

"Yeah, I read that. I had five shark books when I was a kid. Anyway, I turned back and saw the fin coming toward me again. I went under to watch it, watch the whole shark, not just the fin."

The girl squirmed, grinning. "Go on, go on."

She's loving this, Mikey thought.

"Well, it came closer, then went away, then came back. It was smelling me. They can smell things like blood and the oils from your body. I didn't know what to do, so I held the screwdriver out in front of me. Like a knife. Dumb, yeah?"

"And?"

"And the shark checked me out. Came closer, smelling. I backpedaled, pointing the screwdriver at it.

Then for some reason, I screamed. *Yaaaahhhh!* Underwater, I screamed."

Mikey paused, remembering. He still didn't know how he'd thought to do that.

"When the bubbles cleared, the shark was gone."

The girl gaped at Mikey.

"Scared it off." He shook his head, adding, "I didn't go in the water for a month after that."

"That's a great story," the girl said.

"Bill said sharks don't usually attack you when you're close to shore like that. There's lots of fish around for them to eat. But these deep-water sharks. . . ."

Mikey winced.

Suddenly out of things to say, he looked again toward the sharks feasting on the whale. He wondered what kinds of sounds you'd make if one of them ate you. Would you scream your head off? Or would you just let it eat you in silence, knowing it was over?

After a few passes, Bill headed the *Crystal-C* away.

The engines droned on.

Relief settled back into Mikey as the whale shrank to a speck on the water. He thought of death, of dying, of how living things were here, then they weren't. They came and went, came and went. And he thought about how everything—living or not—was just some arrangement of atoms and molecules, the *same* atoms and molecules, everything connected that way. All the same stuff. What makes up that whale makes up me. And the ocean. And the island.

Weird, Mikey thought, the kinds of things you think about out on the sea.

"How do you think it died?" the girl said.

Mikey shrugged. "Age maybe. Or disease. Sometimes they wash up on the beach."

They were silent awhile, standing side by side watching the sea.

"What's your name, anyway?" Mikey said. "Is it Ali? I heard Cal call you that."

The girl grinned. "We never did get around to that, did we? It's Alison. Dad calls me Ali. But I like Alison better."

Mikey nodded. "It's a nice name."

"Thanks. Are you part Indian?" she asked.

"Indian?"

"You know, like Navajo or something."

"No. Why?"

"You look . . . I don't know . . . exotic?"

Mikey scratched the back of his head. "Nope. Irish, English, Filipino, and French Polynesian."

Alison nodded, taking that in. "You about fifteen?"

Mikey turned and grinned, liking that she'd thought he was older. "No, thirteen. How old are you?"

"Sixteen. You got any brothers and sisters?"

"A younger brother," Mikey said. "Half brother. His name is Billy-Jay, for Bill junior, you know?"

"Cute."

"He's . . ."

"What?" Alison said.

"Nothing."

"Come on, what?"

"Well, he's . . . blind."

Alison's jaw dropped, slightly. "That's so sad."

"Not really," Mikey said. "It's just the way it is for him. He was born blind. He doesn't know anything different."

"He's lucky he has you for a brother."

"Me? Why?"

"Well, you like him. I can see it on your face."

"You can?"

"Easy."

"Huh."

Mikey crossed his arms and looked down at his feet. He wasn't used to talking to anyone about anything, let alone about Billy-Jay.

They were quiet.

"You know, he can do things," Mikey said suddenly. "Like he can tell who walks into a room just by the sounds they make. Sometimes I try to trick him by tiptoeing or crawling or something. He still knows it's me."

"Wow," Alison said, in a whisper.

Maybe he'd said too much. But he liked talking about Billy-Jay. It made him kind of dreamy inside. He smiled. You little runt, Billy-Jay.

"He'll be at the pier when we come in," Mikey said. "If you want to meet him."

"I'd like that."

Mikey nodded, studying his feet.

"Can I draw you?" Alison said.

"Huh?"

"Stand over there. Look like a fisherman."

Jeez, Mikey thought. What we do to keep a charter happy. But he smiled inside. Maybe he should take off his shirt and show his muscles. Nah. Too weird. "Can I see it when you're done?"

She studied him, squinting.

Mikey tried to look like a fisherman.

Stand like Bill, he thought.

That was easy.

Alison swept her hand over the page, making large, bold shapes.

"I saw him get born," Mikey said.

"Who?"

"Billy-Jay. My brother."

"You *saw* it?"

"Well, sort of. I was in the room. My mom wanted me to hold her hand."

"Wow," Alison said, still sketching. "How come Bill didn't do that?"

"He was out fishing. Billy-Jay came early, three months early. No one expected it. Luckily it was a Saturday and I was home from school. Mom started feeling something going on. She knew something was wrong. So she told me to get in the car, then she drove us to the hospital. She had to pull off the road three times before we got there. It was scary, I tell you that."

Mikey looked down. "Billy-Jay was so small he didn't look real. They put him in an incubator thing. But he was . . . my brother . . . we had the same blood . . . it was the most awesome thing ever in my life."

He stood in silence. The sun beat down. Mikey could feel it burning the back of his neck.

He noticed that Alison had stopped sketching. She was looking at him again. Thinking about something.

"I can't even imagine," she said.

"No," Mikey said. "It's just one of those things you have to experience, I guess."

"Well, what about Bill?"

"Mom told me to call Jimmy down at the harbor. Jimmy radioed the news and Bill came in early. He had to give his charter his money back. But Bill . . . when he first saw that baby, he couldn't even talk. He just looked at him. He was afraid to even touch him."

Mikey laughed then went on.

"So was I. But now, I wrestle with him. Not hard, but . . . you know. And me and Bill, every day before we come down to the pier, we go in and look at him sleeping."

"Bill does?"

"I guess he still can't believe it. Crazy, huh?"

"No, not crazy."

"Bill said once you have a kid your whole life changes. You see everything differently."

"I guess you would," Alison said.

"Yeah."

Mikey turned to look out over the sea. In the distance he noticed a turbid black mass hovering above the horizon.

Birds. Thousands of them.

CHAPTER 7

"LOOK," MIKEY SAID.

Alison stood and squinted toward the horizon. The black mass moved in surges, heaving this way and that, diving and soaring. Birds swooped down like stirred-up wasps, but more graceful. Some dive-bombed straight into the sea. Small white explosions of white water flashed when they hit.

"Beautiful, isn't it?" Mikey said.

"What are they doing way out there?"

"It's not so far."

Mikey touched her shoulder. "I'll be right back."

When he took his hand away, Alison put her hand where he'd touched her.

He hurried down the ladder thinking, You idiot, maybe she doesn't like to be touched.

"Bill!" Mikey said, and pointed to the birds.

Bill nodded. "Saw them a while back. Take us about ten minutes to get there."

Mikey waited a moment, watching the birds through the window. Bill turned and winked, as if to say, We'll show these guys what fishing is all about in just a few minutes, huh?

Mikey grinned and turned to go back to the flying bridge.

Ernie was playing solitaire, now, half the deck laid out on the table in front of him neat as a tack. His lips were pursed into a kiss as he studied a card in his hand, probably thinking about where to put it.

Across from him Cal was stretched out on the bunk, snoring with his mouth gaping open.

Mikey climbed back up to the flying bridge.

"So what are the birds doing?" Alison said.

"Feeding. They're called noio, and when you see them you can bet fish are around. Aku, kawakawa. We'll be out there in a few minutes, and believe me, you'll be amazed at what it feels like to be in the middle of them."

"Really?"

"It's awesome. Hey, can I see the picture?"

"I'm not finished yet."

There was a snap.

A reel wailed and the stinger line from the port out-rigger flailed out over the water. Mikey lunged toward the ladder.

The *Crystal-C* stopped dead in the water. The boat rocked wildly in its oncoming wake. Mikey hit the deck staggering. Cal got up groggy and sat on the edge of the bunk.

Ernie ran out. "Cal!" he shouted. "This one's yours!"

"Somebody strike it!" Bill shouted from inside the cabin.

Cal leaped up to grab the screaming reel as Bill ran out. He unhooked the safety line and tried to get the rod out of its holder. But the fish was too strong. The rod bent nearly to the water. The clicker screamed and line raced off the reel. "I can't get it out!"

Bill shoved in and yanked the rod out for him, shut off the clicker. He handed the rod to Cal. "Strike it!"

Cal took the rig and drew back, once, twice. He struggled backward to the fighting chair, the rod alive in his hands. His face was pinched and red. His cheeks and eyes bulged.

"Mikey!" Bill shouted.

Mikey snapped out of his gaping and grabbed one of the small rigs. He started pumping furiously. He should have thought to start bringing the lures in be-fore being told to!

Ernie stood behind the fighting chair, shouting at Bill and Mikey. "Let's go! Let's go! Let's go!"

A hundred fifty yards astern the fish exploded out of the sea.

A monster blue marlin.

It leaped full out into the air, its massive sword whipping, trying to shake the lure loose. Mikey stopped reeling. The thing was staggering. It was gigantic. It looked bigger than the boat. Brilliant blue back with shimmering silver sides. Looked to be over eight hundred pounds, way over.

"Good God!" Cal shouted.

"*Reel!*" Bill commanded. "Mikey, they're going to tangle!"

Mikey blinked and reeled the extra lures in as fast as he could, throwing them on the deck. Luckily, nothing crossed the live line. His arms glistened with sweat. The muscles in his wrist and shoulder ached, numb and rubbery. The lures and their wire leaders lay in a tangled mass at his feet.

"Clean these up," Bill shouted. "Get them out of the way."

Bill hurried back to the controls and throttled up enough to turn the boat so that the fish stayed directly off the stern. He pulled back to a crawl and set the autopilot.

Mikey separated the lures, working fast and keeping

low, staying clear of the angler. Cal's face looked as if it would burst, trying to stop the run.

The boat rocked.

Alison crept down the ladder, stopping halfway to watch.

Ernie stood behind the fighting chair shouting at Cal. "Pull! Put your back into it."

"For God's sake, I'm trying to. This thing's strong as a steamroller."

"Mikey, hurry up with those lures," Bill shouted. "I need you in here."

Mikey jammed the lures and leaders into a drawer under the bunk and leaped up to slide behind the wheel.

Bill ran back out.

Mikey looked over his shoulder, focusing on the marlin, now leaping again. Under and up, never in the same spot. Mikey's hands trembled from the excitement. This was the payoff. This was what it was all about. This was fishing, the way he wanted to live his life. Doing this. Exactly this.

The marlin went under.

Cal bent forward, stayed forward.

Bill sponged seawater over the reel to cool it down.

Moments later the blue marlin rose up again and this time it charged the boat. Straight at it. It was insane. Mikey'd never seen anything like it in his life.

Charging, great sword stabbing forward, massive head wagging.

Mikey gasped.

The marlin came at the *Crystal-C* like a deranged torpedo, skimming over the sea completely out of the water.

"Go! Go! Go!" Bill screamed.

Mikey slammed the throttle forward.

The engines roared. The bow rose and the boat lurched ahead. Mikey looked back at the marlin, still charging, still wanting to kill the boat and everyone and everything on it, kill, kill, kill!

Cal reeled madly, reeled and reeled and reeled, picking up the slack in the line.

The *Crystal-C* spewed exhaust that swirled up into the air behind the boat. Bill and Ernie grabbed on to the back of the fighting chair as the boat leaped ahead. Alison hugged the ladder with both arms.

Then the marlin vanished way down under the boat.

Sounded.

Mikey brought the throttle down quickly, then put the boat in neutral, stopping the engines, hoping the line would creep away from the props. His heart pounded in his chest.

Watch the water.

Watch, watch.

No mistakes.

He gulped air.

But for the slapping sounds of ocean against hull, the world fell eerily quiet. Mikey's heart wouldn't slow. He swallowed, took a deep breath. Watch the water, watch the water.

The line slowly moved away from the boat.

"Keep moving!" Bill shouted. "Keep pressure on the line."

Mikey shoved the throttle forward. What does he mean? There *was* pressure on the line. It was taut. Wasn't it?

As the *Crystal-C* once again groaned ahead, the tip of the rod bent nearly to the sea. Mikey heard Cal gasp, trying to stay in the boat, trying to keep the marlin from yanking him overboard. Mikey envisioned the terror of being suddenly pulled into the sea by some terrible thrust from the marlin.

"Jay-zus!" Ernie whooped.

Bill signaled for Mikey to bring the throttle back.

Mikey did as Bill said, looking over his shoulder. He studied the ocean. Nothing out there now but the line, tight as a tow chain. It entered the ocean directly off the stern, squeezing out drops of seawater.

Cal rested, leaning forward. He gripped the rod with both hands, his sides bellowing as he gasped for air. The fish had been on the line for about twenty minutes.

Alison stepped down on deck, but held on to the ladder.

Bill threw a kidney harness around Cal's lower back. He attached it to the reel. "Let your back do the work."

Again, Bill scooped a bucket of water out of the ocean and sponged down the overheated reel.

Line whirred out as the fish pulled away.

Cal started fighting again, the veins in his neck popping out like rope.

The marlin took a foot of line and Cal pulled half of that back. The fish was too strong. Cal would have to wear it down, tire it out, beat it that way. And he'd have to do it before he himself wore out.

A half hour passed. Line in, line out.

Sometimes Cal had to sit leaning forward, having no strength left, forced to watch the marlin steal more line from the reel. Sweat poured off him like rain. Mikey knew Cal could increase the drag and make it harder for the fish. But increasing the drag might snap the line.

Behind Cal, Ernie stood with a bottle of Tecate, holding it at his side, flipping it up every moment or two to take quick swigs.

Line in, line out.

That was how it worked. Back and forth, back and forth.

Mikey did his job. Perfectly. Keeping the line directly off the stern, careful not to allow even the slightest drift to the side.

Bill seemed to have forgotten about him for the moment, so Mikey figured he was doing okay. But looking back from the pilot's seat was giving his neck a crick. He turned away, rolling his head from side to side. All he needed was a neck cramp to ruin everything.

"Mikey!" Bill shouted.

Mikey spun around.

The marlin was charging.

Again.

Coming straight at the *Crystal-C,* but this time underwater. Mikey could see the point where the line met the ocean, racing in toward the boat.

Cal reeled, trying to capture the slack.

"Go-go-go!" Bill screamed at Mikey, his eyes wild.

Mikey rammed the throttle forward.

The boat lurched. The hull shuddered and groaned.

Mikey looked back. The line raced toward the stern, closer. Sickening fear swelled in his chest. The boat would never gain the speed to outrun it. The line was now nearly straight down off the stern, under the stern.

Under, under.

Bill careened in to the wheel, leaping toward Mikey.

Mikey hammered the throttle, but it was already as

far forward as it would go. He glanced back and saw beyond the blur of Bill's hurtling body, Cal flailing back in the fighting chair.

The rod twanged up. Line flapped loose.

Bill lunged for the wheel, shoving Mikey aside. Mikey's cheek hit the window as Bill spun the boat to port.

"He's gone!" Ernie shouted over the roaring engines.

Bill turned back and saw Cal staggering out of the chair, the rod straight up in his hands.

Bill slammed his palm on the wheel and quickly brought the throttle down. Mikey could smell his sweat, feel his heat.

Bill put the boat in neutral and raced aft.

Mikey fell back into the pilot's seat, the boat rocking and rolling in the wake.

Gone.

The blue marlin was gone.

The line tangled and severed by one of the propellers.

Mikey gasped, his lungs bellowing. He put his hand to his cheek. His heart pounded so hard he could feel it banging in his throat. He felt lost, as if caught in a riptide, helpless. Hopeless.

The marlin was gone. The huge blue marlin.

Ernie glanced in at Mikey.

Mikey looked past him at Bill's back.

Bill stood for a long while at the transom, looking into the ocean behind the boat, hands on his hips, sun boiling down.

The silence was as deep as the sea.

Cal, Ernie, even Alison, still clinging to the ladder, stood frozen, as if each was waiting for Bill to say something, do something, bring the marlin back.

Alison stepped slowly away from the ladder. She glanced into the cabin at Mikey and half smiled. Did she know it was his fault? He could not meet her eyes.

Bill leaned way out over the transom, looking into the water. He reached down and came up with a piece of line. He tugged on it, but it wouldn't give. He tossed it back.

"Mikey," he called without turning.

Mikey blew air from puffed cheeks and went aft, out onto the sunlit deck, passing Cal, passing Ernie, without looking at them.

Bill pointed into the water.

"The line's caught in the port prop. Get a knife. Go down and cut it loose."

Mikey's scalp crawled like eel skin before Bill had even gotten all the words out. Instantly, he pictured the deep-water sharks, their bloody mouths gaping, jagged, triangular razor-sharp teeth mindlessly ripping away the dead whale's flesh.

And now, his own flesh.

Mikey looked into the water off the back of the

boat. Deeper than deep. Unimaginably deep. Fathoms of dark and infinite shark-infested ocean. Another world, a place of blood and guts and ripped flesh, a bad dream where you never knew when or where they'd get you.

Or how slow you'd have to die.

Mikey nodded, then went to get the knife.

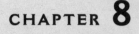

BILL SHUT THE ENGINES DOWN.

Mikey felt it in his ears, the swelling of silence after hours of thrumming diesels. His fear ran wild in the sudden stillness.

He tested the blade with his thumb. Good and sharp.

Cal and Ernie stood back when he came out, nervously switching the knife from one hand to the other. He stopped and wiped his palms on his shorts.

The *Crystal-C* sat peacefully on the water, rocking in the long, easy blue swells that moved soundlessly toward the island.

The ocean whispered.

Mikey could hear it.

Come.

He stepped back, looked up. Turned to see if anyone else had heard or sensed it.

Cal and Ernie had gone back to the table and Ernie was flipping the cards with his thumbs, then rolling them back within his beefy palms. Cal flexed his right hand over and over. "Damn near worked my arm off."

Neither of them said a word about having lost the blue marlin. But their faces told anyone who cared to look that they were flat-out disgusted.

Mikey had never felt so alone in his life.

Did no one care that he was about to die?

Alison stood at the transom looking down into the depths. Her gold hair fell forward, hiding her face. Seeing her brought some sense back to Mikey.

He breathed deeply.

Okay.

He eased up beside Alison with the knife and looked down into the water. It was so beautiful, so radiant, a blue of unparalleled brilliance. It wasn't just color. It was an almost physical feeling, deep and bewildering. Silvery rays beamed up from the unknowable world below.

Alison stepped back.

Mikey sat on the transom and swung his feet over the stern. They just touched the water. It was warm.

He pulled his T-shirt off and tossed it onto the deck.

"What about the sharks?" Alison said. "Like the ones we saw? I mean . . ."

Mikey shrugged, looking into the water.

"You don't have to go. You can say no."

"I have to go."

"Why?"

Mikey thought.

Why?

"It's my job. And Bill. He wouldn't ask me to do anything he thought was dangerous."

Alison started to say more, but stopped.

Behind her, Ernie noisily dug two beers out of the cooler. Mikey looked back. Ernie tossed one of the beers in to Cal.

Cal caught it and sat with it unopened, watching Mikey.

Alison touched Mikey's arm.

He turned back, but didn't look at her. He couldn't. He didn't want her to see his fear. But he was thankful that she'd touched him, so thankful. It was as if he'd suddenly been surrounded by a soft blanket. He wasn't afraid of the ocean, no, it wasn't that. It was that he had to go *alone* that terrified him. With no one to watch his back or his feet, and that's where the fear was, behind and below him. He could almost feel the gaping monster jaws opening, coming up on him, sucking him down, pulling him in. He didn't want her to see his fear.

But Alison had touched him.

He turned toward her.

Her eyes were flooded with worry.

Something Mikey didn't understand passed between them. He noticed that he was gripping the knife so hard his fingers were cramping. He opened his palm, then closed it again around the hard rubber handle.

Then he slipped overboard.

The ocean rushed into his ears, his nose, the warm watery pressure of a billion miles of sea pressing in on every inch of his body. For a moment he heard nothing. But the sounds came quickly, the eerie clicking and snapping of deep water.

It was clear and clean, but the salt stung his eyes. Everything was a blur. He wished he had the face mask, but the old rubber strap had rotted. He spun around, checking for shapes, for moving shadows.

But there was only the soft, empty blueness.

The thought of his feet dangling like edible tentacles made his skin crawl. He pulled his knees to his chest.

Then came up for air. Breathed.

Went back down.

The prop was jammed with a bulge of line around the driveshaft. It would take some time to cut it all away. He'd have to work fast.

Mikey hacked at the bunched line crosswise, pulling it away bit by bit. He sliced his thumb and jerked his hand back. It wasn't a big cut, but it was a bloody one. Brownish streamers wafted away.

He glanced around, all the way around. But he had to finish the job.

He hacked at the line as blood drifted off his thumb, a small watery haze a shark could smell a mile away. He went up for air only when his lungs screamed for it.

Bill was peering over the edge. Mikey could see his and Alison's wobbly shapes when he looked up from below the surface.

Mikey came up, gasping.

"How's it look?" Bill said.

Mikey breathed greedily, his lungs burning. "There's . . . a lot of it . . . give me five minutes."

"Take as much time as you need."

Mikey filled his lungs and went under.

He knew Bill didn't want him to take as much time as he needed, but he'd allow it if it was necessary. That was one of the great things about Bill. He was fair. So Mikey worked even harder, slicing and slicing.

Watching for movement in the corner of his eye. For dark shadows.

He stopped. There! Did he see something?

He spun around. Looked out and down.

Nothing.

Had he imagined it? He didn't think so. The crawling skin came back. The prickles. The warm water suddenly cold.

Fear playing tricks.

Yeah, fear, just fear.

He worked faster, ripping the severed line off the driveshaft until his fingers burned. In his near panic, he just missed slicing his thumb again. But he kept on hacking and pulling until he'd gotten it all, until bits and pieces of fishing line drifted away, suspended all around him.

He burst up and gulped in air, acres and acres of sweet fresh air.

Bill was gone. But not Alison.

He handed her the knife.

She took it and dropped it onto the deck, then reached down to help him aboard.

Mikey grabbed her hand. His arms were sapped rubber, powerless. Blood from his cut streamed down the back of his wrist and stained Alison's fingers.

Bill suddenly appeared. He reached over and grabbed Mikey's other hand and together he and Alison pulled him out of the sea.

Mikey rolled over the transom and fell wet and glistening onto the deck. He lay on his back, chest heaving. The sun warmed his face, the sun that had never ever in his whole entire life felt so good, so hopeful and still. So warm. He was alive. He wanted to lie there and sleep forever.

Alison knelt beside him, Mikey's blood coloring her hand.

Bill said, "When you're ready, set up the rods. Let's get back on the road."

"I'm sorry," Mikey said. "That was all my fault."

Bill squatted down on one knee and said, softly, "Maybe. Things happen. But do us a favor, will you?"

He paused, as if for effect.

Mikey sat up, one hand on the gunnel.

"Learn from it." Bill winked, then stood.

"Already have," Mikey mumbled.

Bill headed back to the wheel. Passing Cal and Ernie, he said, "I'd like to take another crack at snagging that marlin. He may be mad enough to attack anything we put in the water."

Ernie said nothing.

Cal slapped two cards on the table.

Bill went to the wheel and throttled up.

Alison sat on her heels, her arms wrapped around her legs. "You okay?"

"Yeah," Mikey said. "Just tired."

"My dad wouldn't have been so understanding," she said. "And Uncle Ernie would still be wringing my neck." She turned to look back in the cabin, as if hoping they'd heard.

"Bill's the best," Mikey said softly.

He struggled up and reset the rods, ignoring the cut on his thumb.

Bill came aft and put the lures out. Finally satisfied, he went back to the wheel.

They trolled in toward the island, then out again, passing over the spot where they'd hooked the blue marlin. After five passes Bill gave up and headed out to deeper waters.

CHAPTER 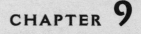 9

MIKEY SAT WITH ALISON ON THE FISH BOX.

They didn't speak, and didn't seem to want or need to.

Mikey's mind and body were numb. His thoughts came and went slowly and without urgency. Noticing things, yet making no judgments about what he saw. Bill at the wheel, studying the water. Cal and Ernie at the table. Beer bottles bright amber in the sun. Second hand on the clock jumping forward, second by slow second. Alison ignoring her father, yet also drawing him in her sketchbook more than any other subject.

Mikey's strength slowly returned, but he was still tired. He could sleep for ten or twelve hours if he had the chance.

He was back in the world now. Revived. But he could still remember the feeling of being in the water. The fear. The aloneness. No one to watch his back.

Forget it.

He looked out at the island, so far away. He wouldn't mind heading back.

He remembered first seeing the Big Island from the *Crystal-C* when Bill had moved them over from Maui. They'd come on the boat. The mountains from the sea were hazy blue sketches in the distance as they crossed Alenuihaha Channel. The island grew clear and brown and green as they got closer, long black fingers of old lava flows scarring the land.

It was only five months after Bill had walked into his mother's life. His mom had married Bill on the bow of the boat. Mikey smiled, remembering that perfect blue-sky day. What a great idea, anchoring off Lahaina with skiffs full of friends watching. Mikey'd never in his life seen his mom so happy, so serene and at peace.

Three weeks after that, everything they owned was packed and stowed all over the *Crystal-C*. Heading out of Lahaina harbor, they looked like the Swiss Family Robinson.

The sun rose as they set out for the island of Hawaii. Mikey'd gone up on the bow and let his face lead, the wind soothing his skin. He was in heaven.

But oh, man, had his mom gotten seasick. So bad she could barely speak. Not him, though. Not even a hint of it. He was made for the sea.

Maybe it was because of the water bed he used to have. His mom had bought it at a garage sale back on Maui. It was just like sleeping on a boat, rocking and rolling. The only problem was the bed had a hole in it. An inch-long stab wound with a glued-on bicycle-tire patch that usually kept the water inside. But sometimes it leaked, and in the mornings when Mikey found his sheet damp, he had to smell it to see if the bed had leaked or if he had.

He smiled, remembering that. He'd never in his life wet his bed. When they left Maui, Mikey gave the water bed to his friend Elroy, whose mother cut it up and made a tent out of it for them. They set it up in the backyard and with white poster paint drew a star and U.S. ARMY on the side. The paint washed away in the first rain, but it was still a good tent.

Now Mikey slept on a real bed that didn't leak. But it didn't feel like a boat, either.

"What you thinking about?" Alison said.

Mikey snapped back. "What? Oh, nothing really."

"Come on."

Mikey grinned and looked out over the wake. No way he was telling her about the leaky water bed.

They trolled south, the island passing by off the port beam, the long, flat empty sea to starboard. He thought about Alison, still wondering why she acted so weird to her dad.

"When you went in the water?" she said.

"Yeah."

"What was it like? I mean, was it eerie?"

"It wasn't any fun."

"Were you scared?"

"Not really . . ."

He stopped. "Yes," he admitted. "I was very scared. My thumb was bleeding, you know? And I thought I saw something. But when I looked there was nothing there."

"Spooky."

"And then some."

Alison studied him, smiling with her eyes.

"How's the cut?"

"Okay."

"Aren't you going to put a Band-Aid on it?"

"No. Better to just let it dry out."

Alison kept watching him.

Mikey crossed his arms. Then uncrossed them. He jumped up and went over to the cooler and got two strawberry sodas and popped the tabs. He brought them back.

Alison took one, still looking at him. She took a

quick sip and grimaced at the carbonation. "Bites,"
she said.

Mikey nodded. "I like it when it's ice cold like this,
don't you?"

Alison smiled. Those pale blue eyes. "Yeah."

CHAPTER 10

THE *CRYSTAL-C* RUMBLED ON.

Alison took her sketchbook and climbed back up onto the flying bridge. Mikey went in and sat in the seat across from Bill. He gazed out over the ocean as they crossed, and crossed again, the great Hawaiian marlin grounds, the seas of massive yellowfin tuna and monster swordfish that some called the best game fish in the world. One of which was lost by Mikey Donovan.

Mikey frowned.

Bill glanced over and winked at him.

Ernie blew his nose, a loud honk. Mikey turned to see him wiping his nostrils with a crumpled handkerchief, pushing his nose to its limits. Mikey turned away.

"Hey, Billyboy," Ernie said, stuffing the handkerchief back into his pocket.

Bill looked his way.

"How do you make a blonde laugh on Monday morning?"

Bill grinned and looked back toward the sea.

"Tell him, Cal," Ernie said.

Cal turned around, big grin on his face. "Tell her a joke on Friday." They both laughed.

Bill shook his head.

Mikey didn't get it. Were blondes supposed to be dumb, or something? Alison was a blonde, and she wasn't dumb. These guys were weird.

They trolled parallel to the island, crossing south to north, then south again in long hopeful meanderings. The relentless rumbling engines numbed Mikey's brain. This was the hardest part, the boredom, the waiting, the endless crawling over waters warmed by a sun that often gave up nothing but scorching burns, salt-cracked lips, and slivers of shade.

Mikey got up and went out onto the stern deck. He leaned against the transom, watching the rods nodding silently to the tug and pull of the lures working in the wake.

As far as Mikey was concerned, the ocean was asleep.

Something hit his back, a wadded-up piece of paper.

He turned and picked it up, then glanced at the flying bridge.

Alison waved at him. "Open it," she mouthed.

Mikey unwadded the paper. *How are you doing?* He looked up at her.

She shrugged and raised her eyebrows.

He gave her a thumbs-up. He was doing fine. Except for thinking about the marlin.

He looked into the cabin.

Cal and Ernie were staring absently out the window. The cards and beer sat untouched on the tabletop between them. Bill held the wheel in loose fingers.

They trolled on.

Mikey was hungry, but since no one else was scrambling for their lunches, he didn't either.

A while later the sky slowly began to lose its blue to the inevitable afternoon clouding, a blanket of gray white overcast that crept out over the sea from the island. Some parts of the ocean were silver and glary.

Mikey fished a root beer out of the cooler and went back in and stood in the aisle near the wheel. He handed the ice-cold can to Bill.

Bill took it, nodded thanks. He sat with one foot up on the seat, his arm hanging over his knee.

Mikey slid onto the seat across the companionway. He scooted up against the window and sat with his arm on the sill, like you would in a car.

The mountaintops on the island were obscured by clouds now. By five o'clock the sky would be white all the way to the horizon. The sea would be silver gray, and the glare off the water looking west would be nearly unbearable.

CHAPTER **11**

CAL AND ERNIE started playing poker again. They said nothing, which was fine with Mikey. There was only the slap of cards hitting the table behind where Mikey sat. The rush of a shuffle every now and then.

Mikey turned in his seat to watch them.

At one point Bill stood and stretched. He pulled the legs of his crumpled shorts down and went back and stood in the aisle near Cal and Ernie. "Nice day, isn't it?" he said.

"Nice boat ride, you mean?" Ernie said, shooting a sour glance at Mikey.

Mikey looked away.

"That, too," Bill said.

How does Bill do it? Mikey wondered.

Mikey frowned and got up and went aft, squeezing past Bill. He climbed up to the flying bridge, where Alison was. Maybe from there he could find those birds again, or a log, or even a skid of flotsam—anything that might help locate fish.

Alison sat as before, cross-legged. She was facing aft, looking out over the wake. Her notebook lay open in her lap, the pen in the gully between the pages.

Mikey saw a blip of a boat far out on the horizon. No other boats in sight. Everyone must be fishing farther south today.

"Sit," Alison said, tapping a spot next to her.

Mikey eased down. "Ever finish that drawing?"

Alison's hand covered the sketchbook.

"I did," she said.

"Well . . . can I see it?"

"I don't know . . ."

"Hey, I can't even draw a stick figure," Mikey said. "Come on, let me see it."

"I guess."

She flipped back a couple of pages and handed the sketchbook to Mikey.

Jeez, Mikey thought.

It looked just like him, but different, too. The face was his, that was for sure. But everything else was sort of out of proportion, larger than real life. It looked perfect that way, though. Grabbed your eyes and wouldn't let go.

"*You* did this?" he said. Stupidly, he thought, immediately after he'd said it.

"Well, no, actually the pen just flew across the page all by itself. It was a miracle."

Mikey flipped back through the pages, looking at other drawings. Some were unfinished, some were crossed out, some had notes around them, and some, Mikey thought, were masterpieces. "This is incredible," he said, then looked up suddenly. "Uh . . . do you mind?"

"You really like them?"

"Are you kidding? This is great stuff."

"My dad thinks they're weird . . . because I don't put everything in proper perspective. He thinks it's cartoony. But I like it this way."

Mikey'd been right. There were sketches of Cal all over the place—Cal in the fighting chair, Cal standing in the stern cockpit, Cal smoking a cigar, Cal snoring on the bunk.

There was one Mikey really liked of Bill sitting at the wheel, squinting, a perfect likeness, his arms bigger than life, sharpened by shape and muscle mass. It was as if Alison had looked for some telling detail about him and emphasized that. There was another one of Cal and Ernie playing cards, their hands oversized, the cards like scraps of paper lost in them.

Mikey flipped to the beginning of the sketchbook. There was a girl with a sleek, long-haired cat in her arms. A massive horse and a rider. Cal in a cowboy hat pulled low. A sleeping dog. A woman scrubbing clothes in a wood bucket. Three cowboys branding a calf, the calf's eyes bulging with fear. A woman saddling a horse, the look on her face one of complete serenity.

"Who's this?" Mikey asked.

"My mom."

"I like it. I like all of them. You're really good, Alison."

"I want to be an illustrator."

He handed the sketchbook back. "Can I . . . can I have one? A drawing? If it's okay?"

She grinned. "Which one?"

"The one of Bill?" He reached over and flipped to the page.

Alison studied it, as if considering if it was good enough to give away. "Sure," she said. "It's yours. But I'll give it to you later. I want to cut it out with a razor so it's not all ratty."

"I'm going to frame it."

"Really? You'd frame it?"

"Of course. Why not?"

"Well, I don't know."

"You're okay, you know that?"

"Good Lord, thank you. I was worried."

Mikey thought he spotted something on the water and stood. There was something that didn't fit.

An off-color blip.

CHAPTER 12

HE SQUINTED AT IT.

They were trolling back closer to the coastline now, where the undersea ledges were, where the current churned and food was plentiful.

Some kind of debris. A dark spot. Cane trash. Or maybe a log.

"Yes," Mikey whispered.

He slid down the ladder and grabbed the polarized binoculars and brought them back up. He turned the eyepiece to focus.

Blur, blur. There!

A waterlogged coconut tree is what it looked like. Two or three hundred yards off the port bow.

Alison moved up next to him.

"It's a coconut tree, I think. Here. Look over there. Keep your eye on it, okay?"

Alison took the binoculars.

Mikey scrambled down and told Bill, and Bill eased the boat that way.

"Bring in one of the outside lines," Bill said. "Replace it with light tackle."

"What kind of lure?"

Bill shrugged. "You decide."

Mikey grinned and ran out to make the change. He chose one of Bill's homemade jet heads. Thirty-pound test reel. He took the rig out and set it up, put the replaced rod in the rack on the side of the boat. He dropped the jet over the transom and let it free-spool out. What was it Bill said?

Think, think.

The drag. Set it too light and it won't hammer the hook into the fish. Too tight, the line could snap. You wanted the hook to sink in as the fish runs.

Mikey placed the lure and set the drag where he thought it should be, prayed it should be.

He stood watching the jet work. Now that he was responsible, he understood why Bill spent so long studying the action.

When he was satisfied, Mikey went back in.

Bill didn't even get up to check it. "Nice job, Mikey. I can tell from here."

Cal slapped his cards facedown on the table and stretched. "What's up?" he said, yawning.

"Mikey spotted a log in the water. I had him change one of the long lines to light tackle. Sometimes you can run into a colony of mahimahi around floating debris."

"Dolphinfish?" Ernie said.

"That's the one."

Cal squinted out the window.

Mikey wondered why they weren't more excited about the log. Floating debris could be an absolute gold mine.

"They don't get much bigger than fifteen or twenty pounds, do they?" Ernie said.

"Thirty-five or forty is not unusual," Bill said. "In these waters, anyway. But the males can get bigger than that. World record is eighty-eight, I think. They may not be as popular as marlin, but I'll tell you this: you can't find a better fighting fish anywhere in the world. Or a better eating one, either. In my opinion."

Cal frowned. "The one we lost was a fighting fish. In my opinion."

Bill nodded. "That it was."

Ernie rubbed a hand over his mouth. He gnawed his thumbnail, his beer-colored eyes intense. "We tracked a wounded elk for two days over in Utah once," he said. "Followed the blood."

"Without a dog, too," Cal added.

"We finally found it dead in a field of waist-high grass. We don't like to give up."

Bill nodded and turned to gaze out over the ocean.

"You're getting us that marlin, right?" Ernie said. "I mean, we're not giving up on that, are we?"

"I'll give you the best I have in me, men."

Cal *humphed*.

"Well, just you remember," Ernie said. "We came here for marlin, all right? Swordfish. Don't waste a lot of our time messing around with this small stuff."

Bill raised his eyebrows. "It's your money."

"Glad we all understand that," Ernie said.

"But what you don't understand," Bill added, "is that marlin like to eat mahimahi, too. Sometimes a log is as good as gold."

Finally, Mikey thought. Bill's getting irritated.

But that was it. Cal and Ernie went back to their cards, and Bill stepped back into his mind.

Mikey went back up to see Alison.

They trolled past the log, three light tackle lures and one long line working the wake. Mikey showed Alison the silvery flashes of light beneath the surface as they passed near the log. Silver glimmerings.

"Mahimahi," he said. "Look. Hundreds of them!"

The *Crystal-C* passed the log again, then once more. Several fish followed the boat, like porpoises, hugging the hull. "They're trying to hide," Mikey said. "Using the boat for protection."

"From what?"

"Marlin, maybe. Probably."

Nothing struck the lures.

Mikey dropped back down to see Bill. "What if we stop and chum, drop baited hooks?"

Bill nodded. Said nothing.

"We could cut up the ono."

"We could," Bill said.

But Mikey could sense that Bill was hesitant to do that. If the one fish in the fish box was all they were going to catch that day, he'd not want to use it as bait. But if they did use it for bait, they might have a shot at four or five mahimahi, if the conditions were right.

"Let's get out of here," Cal said. "Go back to where we hooked the marlin."

Bill squinted out the window. The ocean was silver from the boat to the island now, with the clouding. "One more pass," he said. "Then we'll go."

Cal pursed his lips. He drained his beer and went out and flipped the bottle into the sea.

How could they talk to Bill as if he were some idiot who didn't know what he was doing, as if *they* were the experts? Did it really not bother Bill? Or was he boiling over and you just couldn't see it?

Bill studied the ocean as if Cal hadn't said a word, as

if Bill were in some kind of invisible bubble where insults just bounced away. Mikey thought if someone treated him like that, he'd gct angry.

Mikey went back out into the fresh air.

He glanced up at the flying bridge. He could see only the top of Alison's head.

He turned back and stood at the transom, watching the action of the lures in the wake.

Jumping, bobbing, diving, twirling.

"Come on," he whispered.

They passed the half-submerged tree one last time. Mikey watched it fade away behind the boat.

The engines vibrated hypnotically in the floorboards.

Mikey's eyes hooded over.

Bam! Bam!

Two screaming reels jolted him awake.

CHAPTER 13

MIKEY BOLTED TOWARD THEM.

The two rods bowed out over the transom, bobbing wildly, bent halfway to the water.

The boat lurched forward.

Mikey's immediate instinct was to strike the fish. But Bill had told him he had to give the angler the chance to do it. Some fishermen played strictly by professional game fish rules.

He turned toward the cabin. Cal and Ernie were facing aft, wide-eyed. Bill was looking back over his shoulder, the throttle jammed full up, in effect striking the fish that way. He let the *Crystal-C* run ahead for two or three seconds, then brought her down.

The stern rose in the following wake.

Mikey grabbed hold of the port gunnel to keep from falling. The boat wallowed and rocked from side to side.

Two fish leaped full out of the water, two yellow blue mahimahi, one female, the other a huge bull.

Bill ran through the cabin. Cal and Ernie scrambled up, scattering cards over the table and floor as Mikey waited by the jumping rods.

Bill shouted to Cal and Ernie, "You want to strike them? Keep it official? Your call."

"If it's just a couple of your small fish, what's to be official about? You do it," Cal said.

Bill grabbed one of the rods and nodded at the other, the one Mikey'd set up. "Mikey! Strike him hard!"

Mikey unhitched the safety line, pulled the rod out, quickly increased the drag, and swept the rod back, once, twice. He could feel the hook sink deeper, feel it take hold. The clicker still wailed, the fish ripping line away. The rod jumped in his hands, jerking and pulling. Mikey spread his feet apart and braced himself. The fish stole more line, more and more and more.

In the corner of his eye, Mikey saw Bill striking the other fish. A second later Bill staggered back, the fish suddenly off the hook.

"Damn!" Bill said.

Mikey stood gripping the rod with his knees bent. The muscles in his arms and legs and back were tight and hard as rock. "Who's taking this one?" he shouted.

Ernie scrambled into the fighting chair, motioning with his hands. "Come on, come on, give it to me."

Mikey shut off the clicker and eased back on the drag tension with his thumb, then wrestled the rod back and set the chrome butt into the cup on the fighting chair.

Ernie grabbed the rig, one hand on the rod, one on the crank. Mikey could smell the sourness of Ernie's sweat. "You want the harness?" he asked.

Ernie grimaced and shook his head. He sat leaning forward while the fish ran, taking more line off the reel. He had to stay cocked forward until it settled down.

Mikey glanced into the cabin to check the clock. Bill always did that. It was automatic. You wanted to know when a fish hit and how long it took to board it.

Bill and Mikey reeled in the remaining lures.

Mikey gathered them up. He looped the leaders and moved them out of the way.

"Ho!" Cal shouted. "Look at that puppy jump!"

Nobody seemed to care that the fish on Bill's line had come off the hook. Mikey figured it was because they had marlin on their minds, not mahimahi.

The slowly rocking boat rumbled. Exhaust gurgled and spat off the stern. The sound muffled when the pipes sank low and grew loud again when they rose out of the water.

Alison looked down on them from the flying bridge.
Mikey stuck his thumb up.

She smiled.

Ernie fiddled with the drag until he found the tension that worked for him and finally got the fish slowed down.

He started working it, puffing and gasping.

No one said a word. Ernie held his breath when he pulled, his face red and tight as a screw.

The fish exploded out of the sea, a huge, ax-headed bull mahimahi. It leaped and flapped and shook, then crashed back under and came up again and tailwalked across the sea with sparkles of sunlight winking off its broad glossy flank.

"Look at that!" Ernie shouted.

"Jeez!" Mikey gasped.

The fish went under, then burst out again, shaking its massive head, trying to free the hook. Globs of glinting water shattered and showered out around its convulsing body. You could see the plug hanging from its mouth.

Ernie leaned forward, forced to wait by the ferocity of the fish, the power, the rage. His face was pinched and the sun blazed down on his pinkish white legs and balding head with no hat and no sunscreen. He's going to be sorry tomorrow, Mikey thought.

The fish made a run to port. Mikey ran to the wheel and turned the boat so the line remained directly off the stern. No way on God's green earth was he going to mess up again.

After he turned the boat and saw that the fish had not moved again, he put her in neutral, set the autopilot, and ran back out.

Rivers of sweat streamed from Ernie's hairline, rolling down his cheeks. He wiped at his eyes with the shoulder of his shirt. Cal scooped a bucket of water out of the ocean and poured it over Ernie's head, then toweled his face dry. Ernie shook his hair and seawater glimmered out around him.

Alison sat on the edge of the flying bridge, her feet dangling. Her hand sweeping over the paper. She saw Mikey looking and grinned. She pointed her pen at Ernie and flexed her arms like a muscleman, with a serious-looking scowl.

Mikey laughed silently.

It took Ernie twenty more minutes to get the mahimahi up to the back of the boat.

Mikey stood at the transom with Bill and Cal, looking down at it. The huge bull fish paced back and forth just inches beneath the surface, the line angling back from its jaw, taut as a bowstring. Its color was stunning. Brilliant yellows, iridescent blues. Unearthly greens.

When the leader came up, Bill grabbed it with a gloved hand and slowly pulled the fish closer.

Ernie started to get out of the chair.

"Stay where you are," Bill said. "In case he makes a break."

Ernie tightened his grip and sat.

Mikey grabbed the gaff and handed it to Bill.

The mahimahi seemed calm now, pacing easily behind the boat. But Mikey knew it was only resting, waiting, watching the movements above.

Bill stood with the gaff ready. It was the moment before death, and to Mikey it was always the most painful time, the taking of something so perfect from the sea.

But they were fishermen. This was what they did.

"Take a good long look, Mikey," Bill said. "You'll probably never see one like this again in your lifetime. Not this big, not this colorful."

Mikey thought suddenly of Alison and turned. She was standing now, her sketchbook closed over a finger.

She sees, Mikey thought. She knows.

"What the spit are you doing?" Cal said. "Gaff the damn thing."

Mikey snapped back.

Bill took a breath, then slowly dropped the gaff under the mahimahi's lower jaw, so as not to damage the meat.

He jerked up.

The fish went insane.

It flapped and shivered and shook. Its tail churned

the sea foamy white. Water erupted and spilled over into the back end of the boat, soaking Bill and Mikey and Cal and even Ernie in the fighting chair.

Bill whacked the mahimahi once with the fish mallet.

The fish shuddered.

He hit it again.

Then, with a great surge of power, Bill heaved the bull fish up over the transom, grimacing at its weight, trying to take it straight out of the ocean to the fish box. But the fish exploded free of the gaff and slammed down onto the deck. Cal leaped back. Mikey ran for the port gunnel. The bull mahi was nearly as big as he was, flopping and thumping the floorboards and trying to maim anyone or anything it could get close to. Its mad escape had ripped the gaff out of Bill's hands, and the giant hook clanked to the deck, then bounced up. Its long handle hit Mikey's leg. Mikey winced and grabbed the gaff and tossed it into the cabin.

Cal leaped back again and again, trying to avoid the powerful tail as the fish slammed across the deck like a loose fire hose, *wham! bam!*, flapping, slipping, sliding, careening off the fish box, thwacking the base of the fighting chair, splattering blood and slime over Mikey's feet and legs, the noise deafening, the vibrations in the floorboards monstrous and terrifying.

Bill tried to grab the fish, tried stomping his bare foot down just in front of the tail, but the fish erupted from under his foot. Bill tried to grab it in his gloved hand and the tail smacked him in the face, sending him reeling back.

The lure hung from the mahimahi's mouth. The leader followed, dancing on the decking. The hook looked as if it would break free any moment. Mikey thought it was a miracle that it hadn't come out while the fish was in the water.

"Get a towel!" Bill shouted.

Mikey ran into the cabin and sprinted back out. He threw a towel to Bill. Bill caught it just as the lure cut free of the fish's mouth and sank into Bill's forearm. It went in deeper than the barb. The fish flailing on the leader jerked the hook even deeper.

Bill gasped.

He threw the towel toward the mahimahi's eyes, ignoring the giant hook stabbing into his arm, ripping deeper. Dark red blood drooled down onto the fish and splattered on the deck. Bill blinded the fish with the towel, and the enraged mahimahi slowed and calmed.

Mikey grabbed the fish mallet and tossed it to Bill.

Bill caught it and beat down on the massive head until the bull fish shivered pathetically, slower and slower, hopelessly slower, its life escaping.

Bill breathed deeply, gasping for air. He sat back and took the towel away. Wiped his eyes with the back of his hand.

Mikey gaped at the bloody jaw working.

Open, closed, open.

Immediately, the brilliant colors began to dull, the perfect yellows and greens and electric blue spots slipping forever away, slipping, slipping away.

Gone.

Bill knelt on one knee, head down, still catching his breath. Blood streamed down his forearm.

"Judas Priest!" Ernie said. "Do you know you have a very large hook in your arm?"

Bill glanced at the hook as if noticing it for the first time. He tugged at it, winced. "Mikey, get me a clean towel," he said.

Mikey got a fresh towel and gave it to Bill.

"Does it hurt?"

"Some," Bill said, wincing. "Take the leader off."

Mikey worked the leader off the lure.

Bill took the towel and gently wrapped it around his arm, around the blood and the lure.

He stood.

"Let's get him on ice before the sun saps any weight out of him. I'll be real surprised if this isn't a record fish."

Mikey stared at Bill. He's got a huge barbed hook sunk in his arm and he's thinking about the fish losing weight?

Together Bill and Mikey picked the mahimahi up

and set it in the fish box with the ono. They sloshed what ice they had in the drink cooler over it. Forget the beer and soda pop.

Bill stood back and surveyed the damage in the stern cockpit. A long scar of silvery slime stretched across the deck where the fish had thwacked and slid. Ugly dark red blood splotches marred the white paint along the gunnels and transom. Bill's blood and the mahimahi's blood. It was all over the deck and fighting chair, on Mikey's legs, and on Cal's and Bill's.

In the fish box the dull-colored mahimahi lay with its eye frozen in death. Mikey closed the lid and put the thin vinyl mattress back on top.

He went into the cabin and got the first-aid kit.

Bill removed the towel, soaked blotchy red. The bleeding had stopped except for where it leaked slowly out around the shaft of the hook.

Mikey studied the wound. The hook was sunk deep. He looked up at Bill. "How we going to get it out?"

"Not we, you."

"Me?"

"Hurry up. It doesn't feel that great," Bill said.

Mikey dug the barbed hook out of Bill's arm with a knife sterilized by a match and rubbed clean in alcohol. Bill's face went ashen, but he didn't pass out. The man is made of ice, Mikey thought. He himself would have screamed bloody horror if Bill had done that to him.

Mikey washed the wound with peroxide, scrunching up his face when it fizzed and foamed up yellow. He rubbed a large dab of antibiotic cream over it, then pinched the cut closed and gauzed and taped it.

Bill opened and closed his hand, then nodded to Mikey. "Good as new," he said, then went forward and put the boat in motion. A moment later he came back to reset the lines.

Mikey got the bucket and scrub brush.

CHAPTER 14

THEY HAD LUNCH.

It was one-forty-five, but they'd been busy.

Mikey took his twice-used crumpled paper sack and Alison's clean white box lunch up to the flying bridge. They sat side by side, facing a wake that rolled hypnotically away behind the boat.

Mikey peeked at his lunch. "So," he said. "That enough excitement for you?"

Alison pulled a thick roast beef sandwich out of the box. She looked at it a moment, then put it back and took out an orange. She dug a thumb into it and started peeling.

"Exciting, but brutal," she said.

Mikey nodded. "Yeah."

They said nothing for a while. Alison ate the orange, piece by piece. She put the peels back in the box.

"You don't like fishing, do you?" Mikey said.

"No, it's not that. It's—it's just that I don't like how we are sometimes."

"We?"

"Humans.

"Oh."

Alison smiled. "But it was definitely the most beautiful fish I've ever seen, even prettier than trout."

"Yeah?"

"I think so, anyway."

She paused, then added, "I guess I just didn't like the part where Bill hit it on the head."

Mikey nodded. It wasn't his favorite part, either.

They ate, and after they were done, Alison lay out in the sun on the flying bridge with her paperback book.

"That a good book?" Mikey asked.

Alison thought a moment. "Yeah, it's okay. Kind of boring in places, but it's about the greatest artist who ever lived. You ever seen *La Pietà*?"

Mikey shook his head. He didn't even know what that was.

"Well, how about Michelangelo? Ever heard of him?"

"No."

Alison frowned. "You've never heard of Michelangelo?"

"Well . . . not really."

She closed the book over her finger and shoved her sketchbook toward Mikey. "Write your address in my drawing book. I'm going to send you a picture of *La Pietà*. It's the most beautiful piece of art ever created. It's a sculpture in the Vatican. That's where the pope lives, in Rome."

Mikey wrote his address in the sketchbook. She must think he was an idiot.

Alison grinned at him. "We've got to expand your world some, Mr. Donovan."

Mikey half smiled, not knowing what else to do or say.

Alison went back to her book. Mikey slipped down to the cabin and sat for a while in the seat across from Bill.

Alison, he thought. She was pretty amazing.

"Have you ever heard of someone named Michelangelo?" Mikey said, looking off into the distance. Then he turned toward Bill.

Bill grinned, as if surprised by such an unusual question coming from Mikey. "Sure," he said, quickly regaining a more serious face. "Michelangelo was an Italian artist. Probably one of the best ever. He was an architect, too. What's this all about?"

Mikey shrugged. "Just curious."

"Well, he's a good man to be curious about."

"Yeah."

They had five rigs working now, two long lines on the outriggers and three shorter flatlines in between.

Cal and Ernie talked on and on about the bull mahimahi, about how it had fought with such fury, how it had tailwalked and scissor-jumped and changed directions so fast you doubted the truth of what you'd just seen with your own eyes.

"That sumbuck was a holy terror," Cal said. "Good Lord a'mighty!"

"Was even more'n that," Ernie added. "Just ask my aching back."

"I think you ought to get it mounted, is what I think. Take it home. Or better yet, hang it in your office."

"Maybe I should."

"Oh yeah," Cal said. "One that big. *Gotta* be a record, wouldn't you think?"

"Maybe we could take it home on ice. But that might ruin it. What you think the chances are they got a decent taxidermist around here?"

"Be a stretch," Cal said. "What do you think, Billyboy? Know of any taxidermists worth their salt?"

"I'd say we have some of the best in the world, actually," Bill said.

Cal shook his head. "Maybe. Maybe."

Ernie smirked. "Kind a like asking a used-car salesman if he has any decent cars, don't you think?"

Cal laughed. "Yeah, I suppose."

Bill turned away.

Mikey watched him out of the corner of his eye. What was going through his mind?

"Hey, boy," Ernie said. "Get us a couple of beers, would you now? Make yourself useful."

Mikey got the beers and wiped them dry.

Pried off the caps.

Set the bottles on the table.

He sat again in the seat across from Bill.

Idiots.

Mikey tried to think about other things. What about Bill's arm? Was it throbbing? It had to be. Jeez. Or was he immune to pain, too? Mikey wondered if fish felt pain. Or did they just get mad when they got hooked and feel nothing?

Later, Alison came down from the flying bridge but stayed out in the sun-filled stern cockpit. She sat in the fighting chair, still reading her book.

Mikey went aft and sat near her on the port gunnel.

"I can't even imagine it," Alison said, suddenly looking up. "I mean, getting a hook that big in my arm."

Mikey nodded.

"There's a fisherman here a while back who lost a finger," he said. "Got it tangled up in a wire leader while he was gaffing a yellowfin. The tuna decided to run and took his finger clean off."

"Okay, let's change the subject."

Mikey nodded.

But he wanted to finish. "He just wrapped up the stub and went on fishing," he said.

"Mikey!"

"Right."

He watched the lures. He was feeling better now, not thinking so much about losing the marlin. The water looked cool and clean. Alison was nearby. Sun was all over the boat and ocean. Supreme fishing day. It could hardly get better than this.

Alison marked the paperback and took up her sketchbook. Mikey watched her work on a drawing of a fish leaping out of the sea. Definitely the mahimahi.

A few minutes passed.

Mikey got up and went in to see how Bill was doing.

"Get me a bottle of water, would you, Mikey?" Bill said.

"Sure thing."

Mikey got it and brought it back.

Alison came in with him. "Don't you think we should go back? What if your arm gets infected?"

Bill glanced at the bandage. "It won't. Mikey doctored it up pretty good." He smiled at her. "But thanks."

Cal and Ernie were playing blackjack now.

Mikey and Alison watched.

When Bill told them he had a set of poker chips, they got them out and used them, threatening that they were going to change them into real money at the end of the day. Cal lost almost every hand.

"Where's my luck gone to? You'd think I'd never played this game."

"Forget money," Ernie said, all smiles. "You can pay me in bourbon."

Cal *humph*ed. "You underestimate my ability to make a comeback, little brother."

Alison glanced at Mikey and rolled her eyes.

Mikey laughed.

Neither Cal nor Ernie even once asked Bill about his arm. They could at least have wondered how it felt, or something. Anything.

"Hey, sweetie," Cal said, turning to Alison. "Come sit up here and help your old dad teach this weasel a lesson, would you?"

Alison gave him a look that said You have *got* to be kidding.

Cal said to Mikey, "She's the luckiest or smartest blackjack player I've ever known, boy. I'm not kidding."

"Luckiest," Ernie said. "What do you get if you line ten blondes up ear to ear?"

Cal didn't answer this one.

"A wind tunnel," Ernie said, and laughed at his own joke.

Alison glared at him.

"What?" he said, opening his hands.

"I'm trying to imagine you with a heart."

"What'd I do? It was a joke."

Alison shook her head and handed Mikey her sketchbook. "Hold this while I show this redneck what a wind tunnel can do."

Cal slid over and made room.

"Show no mercy, Ali. None a-tall."

Ernie grinned and dealt two cards to Alison and two to himself, his second card face up. Eight of hearts.

Alison peeked at her cards and tapped the table.

Ernie gave her a card.

Mikey didn't know this game, but Alison sure seemed to.

She tapped again, and Ernie gave her another card, grinning. She took it and wagged a finger, telling Ernie that was all the cards she wanted.

Ernie peeked at his own hand and dealt a card to himself. He grinned.

"Set her down, sweetheart," he said.

Alison spread her cards on the table. "Twenty," she said.

Ernie tossed his cards on hers and swept them all up.

"Ha!" Cal cheered, slapping Alison on the back. "I love you, love you, love you! Do it again."

Alison beat Ernie eight times straight.

"Okay, we're even," Ernie finally said to Cal. "Get her outta here."

"Sure, sure, no problem, *heh-heh*." Cal kissed Alison's forehead. "That's my girl."

Alison gave Cal a hug, then hopped back down to the bunk. She looked at Mikey and flexed her arm.

CHAPTER 15

THEY CONTINUED TROLLING.

Two more hours before they'd head back to the harbor.

"This place is dead," Cal finally said.

How could he *say* that, Mikey thought? They'd hooked a marlin, and a monster at that. They'd boarded two fish, maybe one of them close to record size.

"Yep," Ernie added. "Might as well go on in and see what the dolphinfish weighs."

"All right," Bill said. "If that's what you want. Tell the truth, I'd like to know that myself."

He got on the ship-to-shore and called ahead to let them know that the *Crystal-C* was coming in with what just might be a world-record mahimahi, so roll out the official scale. "And while you're at it, Jimmy," Bill added, "double-check the record for mahimahi. Whisky Bravo one-six-nine-three, the Crystal-C, over and out."

"You got it. Over and out."

Bill started to put the transmitter back on its hook, then stopped. He called home. Mom was there.

"We're coming in early," Bill said. "How's Billy-Jay doing? Over."

The radio spat static. Mikey leaned closer.

"He's better. Don't worry, he's fine. Why you coming in early? Over."

"Bring Billy-Jay down to the pier and see. We might have a record mahi on board. Over."

"We'll be there. Out."

Bill hung up the transmitter and turned down the static. He gazed at the island.

She'd said Billy-Jay was fine. Mikey studied Bill's profile, wondering if he believed it.

They headed toward the harbor, the bow of the *Crystal-C* rising and falling, knifing through the choppy silver afternoon sea. It wasn't so calm now.

Bill wanted to troll on the way in, maybe hook another ono. But Ernie and Cal would have none of it. "Just get us back to shore," Ernie said.

Bill shrugged. "Your money."

CHAPTER 16

SOON THE RADIO STARTED crackling with calls from other boats. Listening in, as always. Trying to judge where the action was.

"Where'd you hook the mahi?"

"Billy, I think the record is eighty-five pounds, something like that."

"Were you off Keahole, or what?"

"We ran into birds off Keauhou, but no action. Where was you at? North end, or what?"

"North of the harbor." Bill gave them that much.

Secrets.

Mikey grinned.

Alison lay on the bunk across from Cal, her eyes and the sketchbook closed.

Mikey pulled his feet up and sat cross-legged in the seat across from Bill.

Bill glanced back at Cal and Ernie. "It's too bad, you know. If this fish does turn out to be a world record, it won't count. It could have made you famous, Ernie."

Bill shook his head and winked at Mikey.

Mikey grinned.

Bill sat sideways in the pilot's seat, one hand loose on the wheel.

Mikey knew he wasn't joking. If it was a world record it *would* make Ernie famous. And the *Crystal-C*. But Mikey also knew it wouldn't count. Ernie didn't strike it. An angler had to fight his own fish start to finish for it to count.

"What do you mean, it won't count?" Cal said, turning around to face Bill.

"Well, the rules are strict," Bill said.

He thought before going on, as if sensing that he should choose just the right words.

"A fish can't be considered an official world record unless you handle it yourself, all the way. Nobody else can touch any part of the rod, reel, or line during the fight. Ernie let Mikey strike it for him. So that would disqualify him. Don't get me wrong, it can still be a record fish. It's just not going down in the books."

Cal turned back and sat staring at Ernie, elbows on the table, fingers laced together.

"Be like making history," Ernie said. "Your name in the fishing Hall of Fame."

No one spoke for a moment.

The engines droned.

Still staring at Ernie, Cal said, "So who's to know?"

Alison opened her eyes.

"Who's to know what?" Bill said.

"Who's to know Ernie didn't strike it?"

Bill grinned, shook his head, and looked away, looked out toward the wake behind the boat, where the sun turned the ocean into winking jewels. "Well, I guess we'd know, Cal."

"Well, what if you didn't tell?" Ernie said.

Bill chuckled.

Mikey laughed, too. Was he kidding?

Bill coughed weakly, a closed fist to his mouth.

"I think you'd better cut back on the beer," Bill said, grinning.

Ernie glared at Bill. "Har-dee-har. That wasn't a joke."

Bill's grin vanished. He narrowed his eyes, as if in thought. He ran his hand over his mouth. "Well, listen, guys, in the first place I don't work that way. But even if I did, and I got caught hiding something like that, I wouldn't be able to get a job pumping boat fuel, let alone continue on skippering. My reputation would be shot. And if I lost that, I'd lose everything."

Ernie huffed, saying, "Who's ever going to tell? Not us, that's for sure. Not your kid. Right, kid?"

132

Mikey looked down.

"Anyway, who's paying for the damn boat here?"

Bill studied Ernie, saying nothing more. He curved his fingers into his chest and scratched, his eyes squinty, as if he'd had about enough of these bozos.

Mikey leaned forward. At *last*, he thought. Bill's going to let them have it. These jokers have crossed the line, big-time. They didn't know one thing about Bill Monks, not one thing. And anyway, who did they think they were? Some kind of kings or something?

Alison sat up, brushed her hair out of her face.

"Ernie's right," Cal said, turning around. "This is our charter, we paid for it, it's our fish to do with what we like. When we get in there and this turns out to be some kind of record fish, then Ernie caught it, and he caught it alone. That's the end of it. This picture coming into focus?"

Cal glared at Bill.

Then Mikey.

He didn't look at Alison.

Mikey felt as if he'd been slapped in the face.

Cal grinned and added, "You so worried about your reputation, well, think about this. Maybe we say you struck the fish without asking us, huh? Rumor like that could do some damage, wouldn't you say?"

Mikey felt his jaw drop. Is he *serious*?

Alison turned toward Mikey, her mouth open. She looked away the second their eyes met.

Bill's gaze locked on Cal. Neither of them flinched. Bill's going to lose it right about now, Mikey thought. And it's about time.

Mikey waited, afraid to even blink.

"Now, now, Cal," Ernie said, putting up his hands. "No need to go in that direction. How about we just throw in some extra cash? Say we triple the full three-day fee? Make the payoff worth the risk, so to speak? I mean, this could make all of us famous, not just me. What do you say, Billyboy?"

Mikey looked at Bill.

Bill glared harder. He clenched a fist and turned away, ever so slightly, his eyes burning holes in everything they rested on.

Mikey stopped breathing.

"A triple fee," Ernie said again. "Ain't nothing to spit at."

Bill started to say something, then mashed his lips into a tight, thin line and turned away.

"Not to mention how much business we could throw your way," Ernie added. "And look what it would do to your reputation, huh?"

Bill put his hand over the bandage on his arm and shifted in the seat. He looked out the window at the sea.

A long, silent moment passed.

"All right," he whispered.

Mikey's jaw dropped.

Something lurched in his stomach, some weird, awful new thing.

No, Bill—

Wait, Mikey thought. Don't jump to conclusions.

Just wait.

Bill has something up his sleeve.

Ernie smiled, cold and flat. "Deal," he said, wagging his eyebrows.

Cal *humphed*.

Bill turned his back on them.

Mikey waited a moment longer, as long as he could stand it. Staring at Bill.

Finally, he got up and went out into the sun. He didn't look at Cal or Ernie or even Alison. He felt dizzy. Stunned. These were idiots on this boat. He hoped the fish wasn't a record at all. But what if it was? Would Bill *really* keep silent? Had he meant what he'd said, *really* meant it? If he had, and if Mikey didn't go along with it, then Bill would be caught in an unforgivable lie and he could kiss his charter boat business goodbye.

Mikey would *have* to go along, he'd have no choice.

He wiped his sweaty hands on his shorts. A triple fee was good money, but . . .

Bill had to have something up his sleeve.

Of course he did.

Of course.

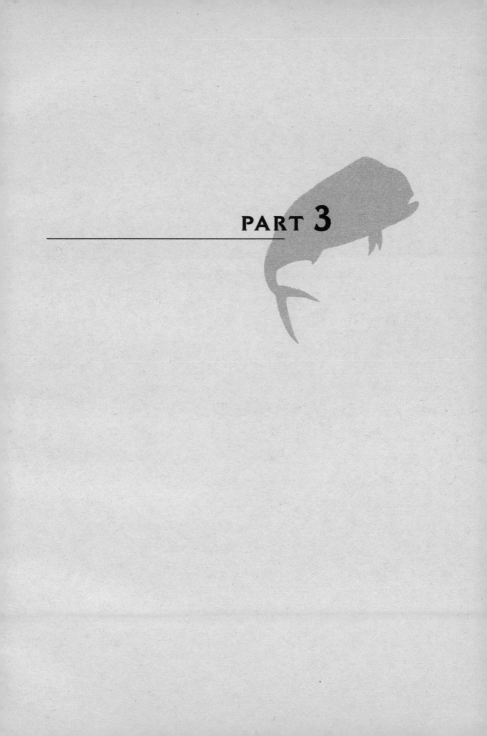

PART 3

CHAPTER 1

BILL THROTTLED BACK as they approached the harbor.

Mikey stood on the bow with the mooring line coiled in his hands. There was a big crowd on the pier, and more people were streaming over from the village, heading out toward where the *Crystal-C* would dock.

Bill circled into the bay. Two fish flags fluttered high on the outriggers—orange and white for ono, yellow and blue for mahimahi.

The sky was a shield of high white clouds, and the water reflected a grayish green in the shallows, the sandy bottom clearly visible twenty feet below.

The slow, smooth motion of the boat easing up to the pier felt right in Mikey's body, in his legs and knees. As it always did.

But that was all that felt right.

His spirits brightened some when he saw his mom and Billy-Jay on the pier. Mom waved, then leaned down and spoke to Billy-Jay, and he, too, waved.

Mikey lifted his chin.

Bill reversed the engines just as the bow was about to touch the truck-tire bumpers on the pier. Mikey jumped off the boat and secured the bow line.

Perfect.

Another small, right-feeling thing, a knot so clean and tight. He ran back along the pier.

Bill, with his bandaged arm, made his way aft and tossed up the stern line and Mikey hitched that off, too.

"Mikey!"

He turned.

Mom struggled through the milling mass of chatting, rubbernecking people, Billy-Jay in tow. "Wow," she said. "Can you believe this crowd? What'd you bring home, Moby Dick?" She hugged him, then waved a hand in front of her face. "*Eew*, you smell like fish."

"Yeah."

She stood back, squinted at him. "What's wrong? You should be leaping with excitement."

Mikey shrugged.

Mom frowned.

Mikey squatted down in front of Billy-Jay. "Hey, bud. We brought you a really, really big mahi-mahi today."

Billy-Jay grinned and reached out to find Mikey.

Mikey took his hand and held it. He seemed fine now. Not coughing or breathing funny. "Yeah," Mikey said. "A giant. Want to touch it?"

"Uh-huh. Where is it?"

"You just hang on a minute, okay? We got to get it off the boat."

Billy-Jay grabbed hold of Mikey's T-shirt, as if not wanting him to leave. Mikey felt like tossing him up on his shoulders and carrying him on board. Sometimes he did that. Bill did, too. But there was still work to be done.

Besides, Bill had something planned that Mikey didn't want to miss.

Cal and Ernie were out in the stern cockpit gazing up at the crowd massing on the pier. They looked like completely different men now, both standing taller. Alison stayed in the cabin, her arms folded, the sketchbook, pencil pouch, and paperback book tucked under them.

Mikey jumped back down onto the *Crystal-C*.

He took up the stern line and snugged the boat up against the bumpers. Ernie, then Cal, climbed off the boat.

"Ali?" Cal said, looking back.

"In a minute," she said.

Cal studied her. He pursed his lips, then raised his eyebrows in resignation. "Well, don't take too long, honey. We're gonna take some photos and I want you in them, all right?"

Alison shrugged.

Cal lingered a moment longer, then turned to follow Ernie over to the fish scale.

Mikey and Bill hauled the mahimahi out of the fish box. A hush fell over the crowd. Bill had hold of the tail. Mikey gripped it by its gills, and together they hefted it up onto the pier. Bill grimaced, and Mikey wondered if it was because of the wound, or if he was just now starting to add up all the problems this particular fish could bring to the *Crystal-C*.

On the pier Bill's friend Jimmy picked up the mahimahi's tail. He threw a short length of rope around it, looped it over the scale hook, and pulleyed the fish up off the concrete, the scale chain clinking and rattling.

Bill tossed the ono up onto the pier. It slid dead-eyed to a stop near the fish scale. No one even glanced at it.

The arm of the scale wagged forward and back, forward and back. It jiggled and slowed and stopped.

"Ho!" Jimmy said, his white teeth lined in gold. "Ninety-one pounds and six ounces. You da man, Billy Monks. You broke the record. You caught Bigfoot."

The crowd erupted in applause.

Bill got off the boat. He took his T-shirt out of his back pocket and pulled it over his head.

"Who's the lucky angler?" Jimmy shouted.

"That'd be me," Ernie called, waving a hand. He pushed closer. The noisy crowd made way, clapping.

Mikey looked down and studied the floorboards. A trail of watery blood ran from the fish box to the gunnel. One of Alison's white shoes had specks of red on it.

"Well, hang on, then," Jimmy said. "I got an official IGFA application form in the truck. We can fill it in now." He whistled, adding, "Man, I gotta call a reporter."

Flash cameras went off as people surged in around the hanging fish.

Cal and Ernie flanked the mahimahi, grinning and waving, bloated as puffer fish.

Come on, Bill. Say something. Do something.

He's waiting for the right moment, Mikey thought. Maybe he's waiting for the reporter, to say it then, say it's a great fish, probably the greatest mahimahi ever caught, but too bad it's not official because . . .

Yeah. He'll do it like that.

Mikey wiped his clammy palms on his T-shirt. His heart thumped in his ears.

"Give me a hand up?" Alison said.

Mikey jumped. "Oh . . . sure." He'd almost forgotten she was there. "Sorry."

Mikey grabbed the stern line and pulled the boat closer. He took her hand. She stepped up onto the gunnel, then the pier. His spirits sank even lower when she let go and looked back down on him. It felt as if something were slipping away. He didn't know what. Something like a friend, leaving for good.

Alison smiled. "Coming?"

Mikey shook his head. "I don't want any part . . . I don't like to have my picture taken."

"Come on, in this crowd they'll never find us."

Mikey hesitated, then dropped the stern line and jumped up onto the pier.

The photographer's rattletrap old Buick lurched to a stop inches from the back of the crowd. He jumped out, his huge belly leading. "Out of the way, out of the way. *Press!*" he shouted, shoving through.

"Press!"

Hidden back in the crowd, and with Alison peeking around from behind him, Mikey watched Cal and Ernie pose. The happy fishermen with their glorious bounty, Ernie's loud shirt open to his stomach, the rod and reel—everything was in the picture.

Cal dragged Bill in for a shot, and Bill went right along, posing beside them.

How could he do that?

They're cheats, Mikey thought. They're liars.

"Disgusting, isn't it?" Alison said.

Mikey's stomach felt like knotted rope. "What?"

Alison grabbed his hand. "Let's get out of here."

Mikey followed her, squeezing through the crowd. He felt dizzy, as if he weren't even in the same town.

It was weird. The whole day had gone from great to shocking to weird and downright strange.

They pushed their way out.

"Where's your brother?" Alison said. "Is he here?"

Mikey looked at their hands, clasped in a tight knot. Alison let go. "Sorry. I just couldn't stand it anymore."

"Mikey!" Mom called. "Over here!"

She was standing by Bill's jeep, waving.

They walked over.

"Wow," Alison whispered. "Your mom's beautiful."

Mikey felt embarrassed. Had his mom seen him holding hands with Alison? She had a grin on her face that made Mikey frown.

"Well," Mom said.

"This is Alison," Mikey said, before she could add to the "well." "She was on the boat with us today."

Alison smiled and reached out to shake hands. "Nice to meet you," she said.

"You must be very proud of your father," Mom said, turning toward the crowd.

"My uncle caught it."

"Well, we should all be proud of this."

Alison smiled, then looked down at Billy-Jay. She knelt. "And you couldn't be anyone but Billy-Jay," she said. "You look just like your father."

"Who's that, Mikey?" Billy-Jay said.

Mikey dropped down next to Alison, one knee

cocked forward. "This is Alison, Billy-Jay. She's my friend."

Alison stuck out a hand, then pulled it back, glancing at Mikey.

Mikey dipped his head toward Billy-Jay, mouthing "Go ahead."

Alison took Billy-Jay's hand in hers and shook it. "Mikey's told me all about you. But you're bigger than I thought you were."

Billy-Jay grinned.

Mikey stood and glanced toward the *Crystal-C*. Bill was back on board. Cal and Ernie were talking to strangers, acting as if they'd known them for years.

The crowd was starting to disperse. Some people stayed to take pictures of the mahimahi. Some leaned against each other. Honeymooners. With no idea they were admiring a couple of cheaters.

"Can we go to the big fish now?" Billy-Jay said.

Mikey turned back. "You bet, bud."

He and Alison each took one of Billy-Jay's hands and walked him over to the hanging fish, now faded to the color of lead pipe.

Mikey bent over, hands on his knees. "It's right in front of you."

Billy-Jay reached out and touched it with his fingertips, then his whole hand. "Big," he said.

"Bill says we'll probably never see another one like

this in our lifetime." Mikey glanced up at Alison. "I believe it."

Mikey showed Billy-Jay the ono, too, and Billy-Jay explored every inch of it, including the eyes, gills, and spiky teeth.

Alison sat down on her heels and wrapped her arms around her knees. She studied Billy-Jay, watching his face register reactions to the fish, the little smiles and moments of thought. Her eyes seemed so kind, Mikey thought, watching Billy-Jay like that. What was she thinking? Mikey became aware of the fact that this was the first time in his life he'd ever gotten this close to a girl. She was older than he was, sure, but that didn't seem to matter.

Jimmy returned with the IGFA application form on a clipboard. Cal, Ernie, Bill, and the crowd that remained gathered around him.

Mikey stayed crouched down with Alison and Billy-Jay, hoping he wouldn't be seen.

Now, Bill. Do it now.

Tell.

Since you missed your chance with the reporter.

That wasn't fair, Mikey thought. The reporter never showed up. Unless the photographer was also the reporter.

"Okay, gentlemens," Jimmy said. "Let's have the facts."

"Mikey," Bill said, suddenly noticing him. "Come. We need you."

CHAPTER 2

MIKEY STOOD AND LOOKED AT BILLY-JAY.

"I'll watch him," Alison said.

Their eyes locked.

Alison smiled, so warm.

Mikey blinked, then walked over to Bill, and Alison followed, holding Billy-Jay's hand.

Mikey was a member of the crew, he had to be there. Whether he wanted to or not. He felt even dizzier. Confusion swirled in his brain.

"Let's start with the skipper," Jimmy said.

Bill dictated the necessary information—kind of fish, weight, length, tackle, boat, time of day, skipper, angler.

Come on, Bill. Tell Jimmy what they're trying to get away with.

Jimmy shook his head. "You men are going to be famous. You'll probably have this record for years before it gets broke. Here, sign this and let's send it in, get her in the books."

Cal and Ernie beamed like five-year-olds with Popsicles.

Mikey glared at Bill.

Cal signed and handed the clipboard to Ernie.

Ernie signed in bold strokes.

He grinned and handed the form to Bill.

Now, Bill. *Now . . .*

Bill took the form and checked it over. He held the clipboard in one hand, as if not wanting to taint both hands. He read the entries.

Ernie held out the pen.

Mikey's eyes riveted on it.

Bill took the pen, tapped the clipboard twice, then signed his name.

Something escaped from Mikey's body.

He felt weak.

Bill held out the clipboard and the pen to Mikey.

Never. Never ever ever.

It's not right.

But if I don't sign, it will ruin Bill.

"Mikey?" Bill said.

Mikey took the pen.

Then the clipboard.

He waited.

Cal and Ernie scowled at him.

"You need to sign the form, Mikey," Jimmy said. "It's the rules."

Mikey ground his teeth and quickly scribbled his name. His hand trembled and his signature was nearly unreadable. Mikey handed the pen and the clipboard to Jimmy and turned away. He felt hot. Anger burned across his face and rose up into his scalp. He could actually feel it. A swelling all over his body.

Cal waved Alison over.

Mikey took Billy-Jay.

Ernie grinned and clapped a fat hand on Alison's shoulder. "So what do you think, Ali? Not bad for an old man like your uncle, huh?"

Alison slipped out from under his hand, looking as if she'd just swallowed a spoonful of diesel fuel. "What I think, Uncle Ernie, is that it scares me to think I'm related to either of you."

Ernie's grin vanished.

Cal scowled.

Jimmy looked confused.

Mikey backed away. Get out of here, he thought.

Alison took Billy-Jay's hand from Mikey and walked over to Mom at the jeep.

Mikey followed, glancing back at Bill, who was now studying the concrete at his feet, Cal and Ernie flanking him, cold eyes glaring at Alison. Or maybe at him. Maybe they thought what she said was his fault.

Mikey turned away.

Alison became suddenly cheery, approaching Mom. "Billy-Jay sure likes the fish," she said.

Mikey gazed at them. Listened to them talk, not hearing what they said. His vision was fuzzy. He rubbed his eyes and turned away, then strode over to the *Crystal-C* and jumped down on deck. He got a hose from the forward hatch and dragged it aft. He reached up and hooked it to a spigot on the pier and turned the water on full blast and started hosing salt off the boat.

He worked fast and sloppily at first, then more forcefully. He shut off the nozzle and took a hard hand brush and got down on his hands and knees and scrubbed the floorboards, working and reworking the bloody spots, the bloody trail, the leftover slime. He never once looked up toward the pier.

"Mikey," Bill called.

Mikey stopped and looked up. Bill stood with Cal and Ernie.

"I need you here."

Mikey set the brush on the gunnel and climbed off the boat. He ripped off his T-shirt and dried his hands on it, swiped it over his face, then jammed a corner of it into his back pocket.

He stood, waiting for Bill to say something. Chew him out for not sticking around, or for making Jimmy think there was something going on that he should know about.

But Bill said nothing.

In fact, Jimmy seemed satisfied with everything. Maybe they'd told him Alison had a bad day, got seasick or something.

Probably.

Cal clapped a hand on Bill's shoulder, all happy again. "The triple fee is yours on Friday, Billyboy, but for today . . ." Cal smiled and handed Bill a crisp, new hundred-dollar bill.

Bill took it, moved it quickly into his pocket. "Thanks, men. That's very generous."

Ernie held a folded ten-dollar bill out to Mikey. Had it stuck between his first and second fingers. "This day turned out to be a bonanza for all of us, now, didn't it, boy?"

Mikey looked at the ten. He didn't want it, but he took it anyway. He didn't care anymore. What was left to care about?

"Thanks," he mumbled.

"There's more where that came from," Cal said, tapping Mikey's shoulder. "If we can do this again tomorrow, maybe we'll even triple that."

Cal and Ernie left.

Mikey looked at the ten-dollar bill. He'd give it to Bill, since he wanted money so much. But later, not now. He'd leave it somewhere for Bill to stumble on. Maybe under his pillow so he could think about it all night.

Mikey stuck it in his pocket.

Bill went over to lower the mahimahi into the back of Jimmy's truck.

Mikey jumped down onto the boat and continued scrubbing—get it cleaner, get the salt off, clean the seats and the rods and the reels, scrub the slime, scrub it away.

"Mr. Fisherman," someone called.

Mikey glanced up.

Alison smiled down on him, hands on her hips.

"Aren't you even going to say goodbye?"

Mikey stood, wiped his wet hands on his shorts. "Sure."

He tossed the brush into the bucket and climbed up off the boat.

"It's not the end of the world," she said.

Mikey frowned.

"Besides," she added, "what can we do?"

Alison studied his face. She reached out, hesitated a moment, then brushed her fingertips down his cheek. They were soft and warm. Mikey smelled suntan lotion. He saw tenderness in her eyes, or understanding, something wise in the pale, pale blue. Her touch fired off a lightning bolt that shot through his body. The feeling grew and gathered in his throat.

"You're a good person, Mikey Donovan," she said.

Alison kissed his cheek, then wiped it dry with her thumb.

And left.

CHAPTER 3

SHE WALKED AWAY BACKWARD, leaving with Cal and Ernie.

Mikey stood gawking.

Alison climbed up onto the seawall and headed back the way she'd come that morning, her hair brilliant gold in the rich setting sun. Cal and Ernie strode ahead, their arms moving in conversation.

Alison looked across the water.

Mikey lifted his hand halfway.

Then she was gone.

Bill and Mikey took the *Crystal-C* to its mooring in the bay. They put her to bed and came back to the pier, all in utter silence. Mikey tied the skiff to an orange float in the small-boat landing. Bill unhitched and removed the outboard from the stern and started toward the jeep.

Mikey stayed in the skiff, leaning forward with his elbows on his knees. He looked down at the half inch of water sloshing around his bare feet. A sketch of moss grew there. He rubbed at it with his heel.

He sighed and pushed himself up and got out of the skiff.

Billy-Jay was in the jeep, both hands on the steering wheel, yanking it from one side to the other. Mom stood ready to catch him if he should fall. Her car was parked in the next space.

Bill lifted the outboard over the back of the jeep and set it onto the rear seat. "Where you taking us, Billy-Jay?" he said.

Billy-Jay turned toward Bill's voice. "Daddy!"

Bill lifted him up and kissed his forehead. He hugged Billy-Jay close, so close you might have wondered if it had been a month since he'd seen him. Bill closed his eyes.

Mom watched, surprise showing on her face.

Mikey stood behind the jeep, waiting. For what, he didn't really know. But whatever it was, it was going to be uncomfortable.

"Daddy!" Billy-Jay said. "You're hurting me."

Bill let go, quickly. "I'm sorry, Billy-Jay. I'm—I'm just really happy to see you."

He set Billy-Jay on his shoulders. "Boy, have you got

to stop growing. You're so heavy you're making me feel old already."

Mom put her hand on Billy-Jay's knee, the look of surprise or concern still there.

"I went to the doctor today," Billy-Jay said.

Bill lifted Billy-Jay's hands off his eyes. "No kidding. Why'd you do that?"

"Mommy, why'd we go?"

"Just a checkup."

"Checkup," Billy-Jay repeated.

Bill bounced him around as if he were a horse, then lifted him off and set him down on the pier and squatted. "So, what'd the doctor say?"

Billy-Jay said, "I got a lollipop."

Bill ruffled his hair.

Mikey felt as if he were somehow not part of this. Nothing seemed real anymore.

Mom touched Bill's bandaged arm. "What'd you do?"

"Just a scratch. Loose hook." He leaned down and kissed her cheek. She put her arm around his back and hooked her thumb in a belt loop.

"Is it bad?" she said.

"No, but I think I'll get it checked anyway, so it doesn't get infected."

"Good idea."

Mom stood back and eyed Bill. Then Mikey. "All right," she said. "What's going on?"

"What do you mean?" Bill said.

"Something's different."

Bill raised his eyebrows. "Nothing's different."

"You and Mikey . . . both of you seem . . . different."

Bill glanced at Mikey. "Nothing in particular. Just men stuff."

Mikey said nothing.

Mom looked into Mikey's eyes, then shook her head and reached for Billy-Jay. "Let's go on home, Billy-Jay. Leave the *men* to work out their men stuff."

Mikey wanted to go with her. But he always went home with Bill. Way it was.

She didn't leave.

Bill took his keys from his pocket. "Let's go show the doc your handiwork, Mikey." He slid into the jeep, started it up.

Mikey glanced at Mom, then went around and got in. He sat with his arms crossed, looking out toward the ocean. Maybe Bill would explain it to him on the way home.

No, it was too late now.

"You sure everything's okay?" Mom said, studying Bill.

"Sure I'm sure."

"All right. See you at home, then. Bye, Mikey."

Mikey lifted his chin, his gaze fixed on the white dot of a boat heading in from the razor-sharp horizon.

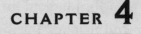

THEY DROVE FOR TWENTY MINUTES IN SILENCE.

Nothing but the whine of the engine and the sticky air, now thinning and cooling.

All the way up the mountain to the clinic Mikey wondered what was going through Bill's mind. He was so quiet. But then he always was. Never said what was on his mind. One of those men who keeps everything to himself.

Mikey's neck cramped from looking away from Bill. He had to turn his head back slowly, rocking it from side to side to work out the crick. His teeth were clamped and his jaw ached. At one point when Bill had slowed behind a truck, Mikey almost jumped out of the jeep to walk home.

He'd never been so worked up in his life.

It surprised him. It scared him.

It messed everything up.

The clinic was a squatty one-level building in a small town way up on the flank of the island. It was yellow, almost green, the color of a painted cinder-block bathroom at some beach park. A surly jungle loomed over it on three sides.

One dim floodlight barely illuminated the parking lot. Puddles of afternoon highland rain filled the low spots.

Bill pulled up and shut the engine down. "Coming in?"

Mikey shook his head.

He could feel Bill's eyes all over him. He turned farther away, so he couldn't see Bill at all.

"Listen, Mikey, there's—"

"I'll just wait out here," Mikey said.

A trembling rose inside Mikey's gut, the kind you get when you're about to get into a fight.

Bill paused a moment, then said, "I was going to say, there's more to that decision than you see on the surface."

Mikey turned toward Bill. "Oh, right. Like more money?"

Bill looked at him. Sad eyes, Mikey thought. He turned away. So what? He was too angry to care.

His hands shook. He'd never in his life spoken to an

adult like that, and especially not to Bill. His throat started to burn. Tears welled in his eyes, but he willed them back.

Bill got out and went into the clinic.

Mikey allowed himself to turn and watch him. He swiped his eyes with the backs of his arms. The trembling subsided. The pressure drained away.

He sat, his mind strangely blank.

In a while, he got out and walked over to the edge of the parking lot. There was a line of concrete tire stops at the edge of the jungle, and he sat on one of them with his back to the weeds and bushes. The sun had set and the sky had darkened. The floodlight reflected off a puddle out in the middle of the parking lot. Mikey tossed a pebble into it and watched the reflection scatter.

He looked down at a string of ants flowing past his foot. They marched silently under the tire stop. He turned and sat facing the jungle, following the ants out the other side and off the asphalt.

Why should he care about Cal and Ernie? They were fools. It was just a fish.

No, there was more to it than that. It wasn't about Cal and Ernie, anyway. It was Bill.

Mikey sat with his arms crossed over his knees. His mind was wearing him out. He rested his head on his wrist.

He jumped when someone tapped his shoulder.

He must have dozed off.

"Let's go home," Bill said.

Mikey stood, feeling embarrassed or sorry or sad. At least the anger had gone, for now. He glanced at Bill's arm, now neatly bandaged and taped. He wanted to ask how it was, and if he had to get stitches.

But he said nothing.

Bill put his hand on Mikey's shoulder and walked him back to the jeep.

CHAPTER **5**

LATER THAT EVENING, after a quiet dinner and after Billy-Jay had gone to bed, Mikey wandered out to the carport, where Bill was cleaning one of his small reels. Mikey wanted to talk. But everything had grown so awkward now. He had no idea how to even start. He'd already said things he shouldn't have, or maybe should have, but said it all the wrong way.

"Mikey," Bill said, glancing up.

Mikey nodded.

"What I'm doing," Bill said, "is changing the drag washers and line. And lubricating the reel. Want to help?"

"All right," Mikey said.

And he did want to help. No matter what had happened, he still wanted to learn. And he wanted to learn from Bill.

Bill handed him a spool of new line. "Always use tournament grade. Don't settle for second-rate line."

"Yes sir."

Bill turned the reel in his hands and shook his head. "I'm surprised this thing's held up as well as it has. It's just about into its granddaddy years. But a good tune-up will bring it back to life."

"Like a car?"

"Exactly, only more important. If something goes wrong with your car, you get out and walk. No problem. But if something goes wrong with your reel when you got a fish hooked up, you could lose the fish. That's a problem, since somebody's paying you because you know what you're doing."

Mikey felt the guilt of losing the marlin flood back. It would probably bother him forever.

"So you got to stay on top of it," Bill went on. "You don't want to lose a customer because you're too lazy to take care of your equipment."

Mikey put the spool down and picked up one of the new washers, turned it over, rubbed it between his fingers, put it back.

Bill took the old washers out, set the new ones in.

The night was still. Mikey could hear somebody's television set. Whoever it was, they had it on loud. You couldn't see any neighbors from their house. Only one small light peeking through the jungle. Mikey wasn't sure if it was a house or somebody's yard light. Everything else was pitch black.

Mikey watched Bill work, too nervous to say what he had to say. He picked up the spool of new line and studied it, smelled it.

"Why'd you let them get away with it, Bill?"

There. It was out.

Mikey stared at the side of Bill's face, at the creases edging his eye.

Bill picked up a small can of 3-in-One oil and thumbed a squirt into the crank. Turned it once, twice.

"It's done," Bill said. "Let's just drop it, okay?"

Mikey crimped his lips, feeling the heat again, the hot thing he hadn't known was in him. *Why is he trying to shut me up, as if what I think doesn't matter?*

Bill wiped his oily hands on a rag. "Let's have that spool."

Mikey didn't give it to him.

"The spool?" Bill said.

The heat burst up, exploding out with a force Mikey'd never known existed before that moment in his life. "How can you just let them walk all over you?" he spat. "How can you just sit there and let them call you Billyboy and let them say the stupid things they say and toss their beer bottles in the water? How can you let them make you roll over like a

164

dog and do whatever they want, even when it's wrong? How can you *lie* for them? Doesn't it make you mad? Don't you even—"

"Enough!" Bill shouted. "Don't you talk to me that way, you hear me? I'm your father, by God, you hear what I'm saying?"

Every inch of Mikey's body shook. Everything was out of control, burning him up, sucking him down. "You are *not* my father and I can say whatever I *want*!"

A deadly silence followed.

Bill glared at Mikey, the dirty rag still in his hands, the muscles in his jaw working. "I think you'd better leave before you get in way over your head."

"Fine!" Mikey spat, jabbing a finger toward Bill's face. He tossed the spool of new line at Bill and spun to leave.

The spool hit Bill in the chest and fell to the gravel. Bill kicked it away. It sailed past Mikey out into the darkness.

CHAPTER 6

THE NEXT MORNING in the kitchen Mikey sat staring at his spoon. He turned it over and let the cereal fall back into the bowl.

Bill sat across from him, just like on any other day. No different at all.

Neither of them said a word.

Mikey glanced up when Mom walked into the kitchen. Her eyes were slightly puffy with sleep. She smiled and walked over and kissed Mikey on the cheek.

Then Bill.

"Morning, men," she said.

Bill grabbed her hand and squeezed it.

Mom took the tray off the high chair and started

setting things up for Billy-Jay. He was really too old for a high chair, but it helped him find things when they were set up within the limits of the tray.

Mikey took a small bite of cereal. It almost made him gag. His stomach was wrapped up tight as leader wire.

Bill gulped his juice and pushed his chair back. "Be right back," he said. "Then we can go."

"Don't you dare wake him," Mom said, wagging a spoon.

"Just a peek."

Mom frowned, but Mikey could see she loved how Bill looked in on Billy-Jay before he left. He was worse than a mother cat.

Mikey wanted to see Billy-Jay, too.

But not today, not with Bill in there.

He got up and took his full bowl to the sink, poured the soggy cereal down the drain. The warm water felt good on his hands. It soothed and slowed his tired mind. He hadn't slept much last night.

Minutes later Bill came back and kissed Mom good-bye, then headed out to the carport.

Mikey waited a moment. Let Bill get out there a ways.

"It's still going on, isn't it?" Mom said. "This thing between you and Bill."

"What do you mean?"

"Something happened between you two yesterday."

Mikey shrugged.

"Can't you just tell me what's going on so I can stop worrying about it?"

Mikey didn't answer. He got the lunches from the refrigerator.

"Mikey?"

"Mom, there's nothing to worry about. Anyway, I don't want to talk about it."

He took the lunches out to the jeep, forgetting to stop the screen door from slapping behind him. How could he explain it to her when he couldn't even explain it to himself?

He set the lunches in the jeep, then went into the carport and took out the ice, refilled the bucket and set it back in the freezer, got the beer and soda and water and set them all on the backseat.

Mom stood in the light of the open door, one hand holding it back.

Bill and Mikey got in the jeep and drove down to the pier and parked and got out. Mikey still hadn't said one word to Bill.

Bill took the outboard and Mikey fumbled with the ice. This time he kept it in the burlap bag, not caring if anyone thought that was a sissy way to carry it. Should have done that the first time.

Out in the harbor, Mikey sat gripping the sides of the skiff as it slipped past silent moored boats that loomed over them like sleeping whales. One boat had a hull marred by dark rust lines that ran down from its deck holes, the stains ignored by its skipper, as if that part of the boat didn't matter. If that was my boat, Mikey thought, I'd scrub them away.

He sat in the skiff facing forward, imagining Bill behind him with one hand on the outboard throttle. Mikey wondered if Bill noticed the rust lines, too.

Probably.

Bill hadn't said a thing about last night. Fine, Mikey thought. He didn't want Bill to bring it up, anyway. What he wanted was to forget it ever happened. The whole thing scared him. It wasn't supposed to be like that with Bill.

None of it was supposed to be this way.

Yet it was.

Mikey gazed up at the purple gray sky, then out over the ocean, so calm, so glassy. It was the stopped time, a relief, a time before boats coughed to life. Before tourists, beer, box lunches, boiling sun and all the boasting talk.

He liked this time best of all.

Even though the 10-horse outboard shattered the stillness, it was part of what the harbor was. The sound belonged there. Like a boat's clock bell. Like the salt taste in the air. Like the smell of diesel. Like Bill, and the *Crystal-C*.

Mikey puffed up his cheeks and let the air out.

The day had just begun and already he was tired. He

felt as if the life were sapped out of him. He slapped his cheek lightly, hoping that would snap him awake.

When they got to the boat, Bill stepped aboard with the ice, and Mikey worked the skiff to the buoy, tied it off, and climbed aboard the *Crystal-C*.

He waited.

The whole world was silent now. Just the gentle lapping against the hull and distant hush of small waves sweeping over the rocky shore.

How can I do this? How can I listen to one more dumb joke? But Alison would be there.

Bill fired up the boat. "Cut her loose," he called.

Mikey threw the mooring line into the skiff.

Bill throttled up and eased the *Crystal-C* toward the pier. The engines vibrated through Mikey's bare feet. A boat was more than a boat. It was the air he breathed.

To fish.

To skipper.

To be a man of the sea.

And now he couldn't even stay awake.

Mikey noticed his teeth clamped tight. He opened his mouth and worked his lower jaw from side to side, trying to relax.

Breathe.

They tied the boat at the pier. Mikey did his job. Wiped the salt off the seats and windows. Fleeced the rods and reels. Chipped the ice, stocked the drink cooler. Swept the spotless deck.

Bill checked the lures.

The engines idled, rumbling low and familiar. The sunrise, still behind the mountain, had begun to lighten the sky so that the island now stood in stark silhouette.

When the work was finished, Mikey climbed off the boat. He sat on the wooden rail that edged the pier, arms crossed over his knees, gazing around the harbor at the few early lights freckling the village. They'll come down along the seawall, he thought. Like yesterday. She'll be following them.

Now nothing moved but the low swells quietly rising and falling against the rocks below the sea wall.

Alison.

She was the one good thing he had to look forward to. If she didn't come, could he even go out? How many more "Billyboys" could he take?

At first they were only shadowy shapes. Then he could make them out distinctly, Cal, Ernie . . .

She wasn't with them.

Mikey's spirits flattened. He stood and squinted into the vagueness back where the seawall began, searching the shapes, the shadows.

Nothing.

He glanced toward the boat.

The cabin was an envelope of light in the darkness.

Bill was rummaging through his lure drawer, just the top of his head visible.

"They're coming," Mikey called.

Bill looked up, nodded.

Cal and Ernie approached, two dark shapes bobbing as they walked.

Mikey took up the stern line and pulled the *Crystal-C* closer to the pier so they could climb aboard.

They nodded to Mikey, one after the other. Cal handed Mikey two six-packs of Tecate, then stepped down onto the boat and turned, and Mikey handed the beer back to him.

No words. No smiles or good mornings or friendly fisherman's chat. Let's go. We got fish to catch. We're burning daylight.

Mikey dropped the stern line, glancing one last time toward the seawall.

The engines rumbled low and deep. Cal laughed inside the cabin. A pickup truck pulled onto the pier and parked. A man got out and threw a coiled hose over his shoulder. Another skipper.

Down in the lighted cabin, Mikey could see Ernie rubbing his hands together, all fired up and ready to go.

"Damn good fighter, that dolphin fish was," Mikey heard him say to Bill, so loud it sounded as if he were shouting. "Cal'd like a shot at one, too, wouldn't you, Cal?"

"Is the pope Catholic?"

"Hear that, Billyboy?"

Bill peeked past Ernie and nodded for Mikey to get the ropes and jump aboard.

How can I? Mikey thought.

But he untied the *Crystal-C* and dropped the ropes on deck. He leaned out over the gap and pushed the boat away from the pier, then stepped aboard.

Bill brought the throttle up, slow and easy.

The *Crystal-C* rumbled slowly out into the harbor.

Mikey looped and stowed the dock lines. Usually this was a time when he liked to go in and listen to the anglers chattering, all excited about the new day.

But today he stayed out in the stern cockpit. He sat on the starboard gunnel, looking back at the dark island.

After they'd cleared the harbor, Cal came out onto the stern deck, tapping a roll of paper on his palm. He squinted at Mikey. Today he wore a T-shirt that said BUY ME ANOTHER DRINK, YOU'RE STILL UGLY on the front. A fresh cigar glowed in the corner of his mouth.

"Ali wanted me to give this to you," he said, still tapping the rolled-up paper.

Mikey stood.

A fluff of burning tobacco ash fell onto the roll, and Cal quickly brushed it away, scowling.

Mikey waited, wanting what Alison had sent him.

A bright red ribbon held it closed. Mikey hadn't noticed Cal bringing it aboard.

When Cal didn't hand it to him, Mikey said, "What is it . . . sir?"

"One of her drawings, I suppose."

Cal sucked in on the cigar. The tip glowed bright. He let the smoke out in Mikey's direction, not in his face, but close, his eyes steady, unmoving. He tapped the roll on his palm one last time, then handed it to Mikey.

"Thank you, sir," Mikey said.

He didn't look at it at first, trying to keep his eyes on Cal, because Cal was looking at him weird, his gaze never wavering.

Mikey blinked, then looked down at the rolled-up paper. It was in pristine condition. Smooth and clean. Mikey wanted to unroll it right then and there, but not with Cal standing over him like that.

Cal didn't leave.

"She's a handful, my Ali. But that girl has a God-given talent."

"Yes sir," Mikey said.

Cal removed the cigar and blew out another stream of smoke, this time shooting it out the side of his mouth.

Then he *humphed*, and went back into the cabin.

Mikey took a deep breath.

Cal stopped and glanced one more time at Mikey, then turned back, saying, "So where we headed today, Billyboy?"

Mikey ran his hand along the paper. The ribbon was tied perfectly, not rolled over or crushed. He tugged a loose end and the bow fell apart. The paper spun wider in his hands.

"All right, men!" Ernie all but shouted.

Mikey looked up. Ernie and Cal were crowded around Bill, up at the wheel.

Ernie clapped Bill on the shoulder. "Let's do it! We're gonna snag that marlin again, I just know it, I can feel it in my blood!"

Mikey turned away and sat back on the gunnel.

The hum of the engines sliced through the cool morning air, the boat riding easy on the flat sea. They were traveling parallel to the coastline now, heading out toward the point.

Mikey held on to the tingling feeling of not knowing what Alison had sent him. Carefully, slowly, he unrolled the paper.

There were three drawings—two magazine-sized and one about the size of a postcard. There was something written on the small one. A note. He quickly turned it over. Save that one for last.

The first of the larger drawings was the one of Bill with the big-muscled arms, the one he'd wanted.

The other was of him and Billy-Jay, squatting down. Billy-Jay was touching the striped ono. Mikey focused on Billy-Jay's hands, his eyes went straight to them. The drawing just naturally took him there. That was what Alison had pinpointed, Billy-Jay's hands.

He studied both drawings, looking over every detail. When he couldn't wait any longer, he turned the small one over.

It was sketched in black ink with a fine-point pen on slightly thicker paper. High-quality paper.

It was of him.

He was standing on the flying bridge, squinting into the sun with his hand under his T-shirt, scratching his chest. On the shirt it said INTREPID, with the jumping marlin under it. And below that Alison had added *Skipper: Mikey Donov—*. The rest of it was lost in the folds around his arm.

At the bottom in small, clean print was a note.

*If we lived in the same town we'd be friends. I know
we would. I don't think I'll ever, ever forget you,
Mikey Donovan.*

Love,

Alison

Mikey turned toward the island.

The pier grew smaller and smaller as the boat

knifed toward open sea, the slight roll of the hull hypnotic and familiar.

I won't forget you either, Alison Flynn.

He turned and looked in at Bill, sitting sideways in the pilot's seat, his back against the window. One hand on the wheel. Silent. A steaming mug of coffee. Thinking whatever it is that Bill Monks thinks.

Cal and Ernie were now at the table, breaking out the cards. Coffee, cigars, poker chips.

Mikey rolled the three drawings back up and retied the ribbon, then took them and carefully nestled them into the towel drawer across from Cal and Ernie.

Ernie flicked cards to Cal and himself, eyes squinting against the smoking cigar pinched between his teeth. "All right, let's see how well you can do without your little girl and her luck."

Cal *humph*ed. "You're running on empty, little brother."

Ernie chuckled, then glanced at Mikey. "You practice your boat handling last night, boy?"

Cal shook his head, grinning.

Mikey made his way forward, not letting his face change in the slightest way.

Bill turned, noticing Mikey approaching.

Mikey wondered if he'd been thinking about last night in the carport. Mikey felt bad about that. Really bad.

"Bill," Mikey said. "About last—"

"It's forgotten, Mikey."

Mikey studied Bill's face, the creases around the eyes, the smooth, sun-dark skin and small chin scar. For the first time Mikey noticed a slight graying at Bill's temples.

Bill smiled. "Believe it or not, Mikey, I was thirteen years old myself once. I believed something was either right or it was wrong, and that there was no in-between." Bill paused, then looked down and said, "Well, there is an in-between, Mikey."

What did that mean?

Mikey pursed his lips. "I'm really sorry, Bill, really. But I can't do this, not with these . . ."

He turned toward Cal and Ernie. When he saw them looking, he turned back.

"Can't do what, son?"

The word *son* threw him. He hesitated.

"It's just . . . it's just . . . *wrong*, Bill. What they did is wrong and I can't go along with it. I'm sorry."

Bill turned away, looking toward the horizon. He rubbed a hand over the back of his neck.

"Why are you letting it bother you so much?" he said softly. "It's my problem, Mikey. Not yours. It shouldn't matter to you."

"But it *does* matter."

"Why does it matter, Mikey?"

Mikey had no figured-out answer for that. It was

just something he felt. "I—I don't know," he finally said. "It just does, that's all."

"Well, I'm not turning around and taking you back."

"I'm not asking you to take me back."

Bill frowned. "Well, what are you asking?"

Mikey looked into Bill's eyes, not knowing what to do, what to say. His throat was on fire, about to explode. He hated this.

Bill sipped his coffee, studying Mikey over the rim.

Mikey studied him back.

When Bill dropped his gaze, Mikey did, too, then turned and made his way aft.

Out on the dark stern deck, he glanced back into the lighted cabin. Bill, Cal, and Ernie were all watching him. They seemed curious, or maybe amused.

Mikey glanced toward the rocky shoreline, passing by less than a hundred yards away, shadowy in the murky light.

He looked back in at Bill.

Then he jumped overboard.

Immediately, the *Crystal-C* slowed, then stopped. The stern rose and settled.

Bill ran out. "Mikey!"

The ocean was warm and luxurious. It filled Mikey's ears and flooded his eyes, so soft, so clean. He wiped a hand over his face.

Cal and Ernie came aft, too, but not so fast. They flanked Bill, Ernie with his hands on his hips, Cal squinting with the cigar in the middle of his mouth.

Mikey watched them, wondering what Bill would do.

Cal took the cigar out and held it down at his side, never taking his eyes off Mikey, and Mikey marveled at the view from so low in the water, all of them seeming so distant now, looking down on him.

The *Crystal-C* sat purring on the water, waiting. The outriggers stabbing the dawn sky.

Ernie shook his head and went back into the cabin. Cal threw his cigar in the water and followed a moment later.

Bill stayed where he was.

What was he thinking? Did he care? Was he angry?

It really was amazing how much he looked like Billy-Jay.

Mikey started swimming away on his back, slowly, his eyes on Bill. He felt confused and restless and empty, just as he had trying to sleep last night. He hadn't planned to jump off the boat. Why'd he do it?

Bill.

He seemed so alone now.

It occurred to Mikey that it had been like that every day of the charter. He'd been with Cal and Ernie, yet never with them at all, not even once.

It hadn't been like that with other charters.

His heart suddenly flooded with sadness. And gratitude, too, for Bill. And for how Bill felt about Mom. And for how Billy-Jay would never have to worry about anything in his whole life as long as Bill was around.

Bill turned to go back into the cabin.

"Wait," Mikey whispered.

He kicked up in the water and waved and shouted. "Bill, wait! Come back! *Dad!*"

Bill stopped and turned, his lips parted.

He walked back to the transom, the worry draining away from his face. Never taking his gaze off Mikey, he leaned forward and pointed.

At Mikey.

Just pointed.

"I'll—I'll be there to clean up when you get in, okay?" Mikey called. "Okay? I'll be there."

Bill cupped his hands around his mouth. "I'm counting on it."

Then he turned and strode back through the cabin, passing Cal and Ernie without a glance. He slid into the pilot's seat and throttled up.

The *Crystal-C* slipped around the point.

Engines thrumming.

Fading away, fading away.

Mikey floated.

His hands and feet barely moved.

All he could see of the *Crystal-C* now were the outriggers and the top of the flying bridge, moving away around the point.

What have I *done*?

Why did . . .

"Come back!" Mikey shouted. "Bill! Come *back*!"

But there was nothing there now—no thrumming, no outriggers, no flying bridge—nothing but the long, sharp horizon and empty sky.

Gone.

He looked back toward the harbor. Scattered morning lights woke in the dark hotels and bobbed above the water.

Mikey turned and slowly swam toward shore.

His arms felt weak and his throat burned.

He swam between the rocks into a small cove. Water streamed from his legs as he stumbled up onto the beach, his shirt and shorts clinging to his body. He dropped down onto the sand and lay back with his face to the sky.

And closed his eyes.

Only moments later, it seemed, he woke with the new sun sprinkling down all around him.

ABOUT THE AUTHOR

GRAHAM SALISBURY's family has been in the Hawaiian Islands since the early 1800s. He grew up on Oahu and on Hawaii. He graduated from California State University and received an M.F.A. from Vermont College of Norwich University. He lives with his family in Portland, Oregon.

His first novel, *Blue Skin of the Sea*, won the Bank Street Child Study Association Children's Book Award, the Judy Lopez Award, and the Oregon Book Award and was selected as an ALA Best Book for Young Adults. *Under the Blood-Red Sun* won the Scott O'Dell Award for Historical Fiction, the Oregon Book Award, Hawaii's Nene Award, and the California Young Reader Medal, was an ALA Notable Book and Best Book for Young Adults, and is on many state award lists. *Shark Bait* was selected for the Oregon Book Award and was a *Parents' Choice* Silver Honor Book. *Jungle Dogs*, his most recent novel, was an ALA Best Book for Young Adults.

Graham Salisbury has been a recipient of the John Unterecker Award for Fiction and the PEN/Norma Klein Award.

The author would like to thank John Honl for giving him a life on the sea.